FALLING ON MAIN STREET

TARA GRACE ERICSON

SILVER FOUNTAIN PRESS

Tara Grace Ericson

Revised 2020.
Original Copyright © 2018
Tara Grace Ericson and Silver Fountain Press
All rights reserved.

This book is a work of fiction. The names, characters, places, and incidents are products of the writer's imagination or have been used fictitiously and are not to be construed as real. Any resemblance to persons, living or dead, actual events, locale or organizations is entirely coincidental. The author does not have any control over and does not assume any responsibility for third-party websites or their content.

Paperback ISBN-13: 978-1-949896-01-5
Ebook ISNB-13: 978-1-949896-00-8

CONTENTS

To my husband, without whose support this novel would have never happened and who co-stars in my favorite love story of all: ours.

Trust in the LORD with all your heart and lean not on your own understanding; in all your ways submit to him, and he will make your paths straight.

Proverbs 3:5-6

1

Taking refuge behind a mannequin, Charlotte Walters stared at her designer shoes and tried to catch her breath. "Can I help you find something?" The amused tone of a store employee made Charlotte close her eyes tightly. *Could this moment get any more humiliating?* Charlotte opened her eyes, lifted her chin, and returned to full height from her crouched position behind the awkwardly posed plastic body. A quick glance around the store revealed her impromptu escape route had landed her in an outdoors specialty store. The mannequin she hid behind? Decked head to toe in camo, neon orange, and denim—A far cry from Charlotte's silk shirt, pencil skirt, and Jimmy Choos.

She turned to the young man and glanced at his nametag

"Thank you, Brandon. I'm fine." Brandon raised his eyebrows and gave a polite nod. When the employee turned away, Charlotte's shoulders sagged. The effort of putting on a brave face, even for a minute, exhausted her. Maybe her therapist was right. Dr. Watts insisted that staying in her condo, right around the corner from the Millennium offices, was contributing to her anxiety attacks. To prove him wrong, today she'd ventured out for something other than the therapy appointments for the first time in a month. An entire month of twice-weekly therapy sessions and she was no closer to her old self than she had been on day one.

Cautiously, she looked out the store window to see if the reason for her hiding was gone. Just a moment ago, Charlotte spotted the former client a block away in the small shopping promenade and panicked, dashing into the nearest store. She stuck out like a ringing cell phone in a library among the hunting gear.

The coast was clear and Charlotte swallowed the nausea that flared at the thought of venturing back outside. Maybe Dr. Watts was on to something. What if she went somewhere no one would know her? She'd thought him a quack when he first suggested it.

"Just get out of town for a while."

When Charlotte questioned how the heck to do that; he had responded, "Just drive until you run out of gas and stay there. You'll know when you get there." At Charlotte's wide eyes and gaping mouth, he continued. "Leave your stuff. Being in this city won't help you."

His eyes had softened and Charlotte saw the compassion in them. "There's more to life than work, Charlotte."

With one more defeated glance back at the hunting goods store and the young clerk who still watched her from a display near the wall; Charlotte pushed the door open and prepared for the walk back to her condo. If she worked quickly, she could leave tomorrow.

CHARLOTTE PULLED into the station off Highway 40 in Indiana running on fumes, literally and emotionally. She studied the small gas station, with its old fuel pumps and faded Coca-Cola sign. *I may have gotten out of Dodge, but I'm not exactly sure the*

middle of nowhere will work for me. At least she still had music; the radio station she picked up in Terre Haute remained strong. Charlotte spent the last hour belting out twangy country songs she hardly knew the words to. *Might as well get into my new lifestyle,* she thought wryly.

Life out here couldn't be more different from her work as a top-tier recruiting consultant for companies around the world. Until recently, her reputation was flawless. Charlotte had something few others did: she could read potential employees like an open book. Looking for someone to overhaul a company? Charlotte could tell in one interview if an applicant is genuinely creative, bold, and progressive; or if they have been claiming others' ideas as their own. The insecurities and skeletons buried beneath power suits or carefully applied eyeshadow always came to light. Candidates she approved for a position **always** lasted and **always** performed. It didn't hurt that her stock portfolio was full of companies on the brink of disaster until the right person came into power.

That had been her world. And here she was, standing beside her black Mazda sports car pumping a few more dollars into the tank on the side of the highway in Indiana. Indiana! She'd never been to Indiana, other than Indianapolis. *I must be crazy.* That was the rumor, at least. Crazy Charlotte. Washout Walters. Ugh. Even as it made her cringe, she was determined not to care anymore. For the next year, no one could touch her.

Charlotte walked inside the "QuikStop" to pay for her gas, having realized there was no card reader on the pump. *Where am I - the eighties?*

"Hi there, darlin'," the clerk said with a warm smile, "anything other than the gas today?"

Taken aback by the friendly greeting, Charlotte stuttered. "Uh... I don't think so. Unless you have a local newspaper?"

The shopkeeper shook his head and clucked his tongue. "Paper in Minden don't come out 'cept on Tuesdays, but I think I've still got a copy of last week's if you want it."

Charlotte resisted the urge to gasp. A weekly newspaper? She started every day with a copy of the USA Today, Wall Street Journal and the St. Louis Post Dispatch. Or at least, she used to.

Shaking off the unwelcome reminder of the world moving on without her, she nodded. "Sure, thanks, that'd be great."

As the clerk retrieved the newspaper from under the counter and rang her up, Charlotte let her mind wander. *What could I possibly find to do here? Maybe this wasn't such a good idea...*

"Anything in particular you looking for in the newspaper?" Curiosity was etched on the clerk's face as if labeled with a sharpie.

Charlotte jerked a shoulder and glanced at the front page. "Maybe a job, a place to rent?"

"Well, you should have said something!" His sudden volume change startled her. "I know Miss Ruth has been looking for someone to rent her cabin. Want me to ask her for ya?"

Charlotte took a step back from the counter and reached for her change. "Umm, no, that's okay. I'm sure I can find something on my own."

He eyed her. "Well, alright then. Let me know if you change your mind. Miss Ruth would sure appreciate it. And you can't beat that cabin! I'd rent it myself if I didn't have my place to consider."

"I will, thanks."

Charlotte turned and walked out the door, still processing. *A cabin? Surely, someone has an apartment around here, right?* If she couldn't find a place to stay, she'd have to keep driving. Something felt good about this place, though. The friendliness of the clerk, even the cool breeze gave her the feeling this was the place she'd get better.

She climbed back into the front of her Mazda and pulled her sunglasses from their perch on her head as a mud-caked pickup truck pulled in the pump next to her. It might have been green at some point. Charlotte stared through her sunglasses and watched a teenager climb out of the cab in jeans and a faded red baseball cap. He had grease and dirt smudged on his face as he eyed her Mazda with obvious appreciation. In response, she revved the engine and pulled out of the lot.

At the next cross street, Charlotte turned off the highway where a small green sign announced the town. Minden: Population 2340. She crept past "Bud and Janine's Café" and a little store with a battered old sign that simply read "Hardware". A bar and grill announced itself with the universal neon accessories. *Guess some things aren't so different from the city.*

There was a pretty little building that had a black sign with gold lettering declaring it "Minden Funeral Home". It was next door to "Minden State Bank", and the "Minden U.S. Post Office". She also spotted a small bakery and a craft store. The street was lined with carefully tended potted plants, and the street lights had patriotic banners still displayed from the Fourth of July celebration nearly two months earlier.

Then, as she crossed Elm, the landscape switched. Little houses with white picket fences. Trellis gates with ivy climbing the sides. Bright green lawns and friendly looking shutters on the windows. There were hanging pots and porch swings, weeping willows, and clothes drying in the breeze. It was perfect. *Exactly what I need. This couldn't be farther away from the city life I'm used to.* She rolled down the window and breathed deep. *A little R&R in Mayberry and I can go take my life back.*

Charlotte turned the car around when she reached the Minden Town Park at the dead end of Main Street and went back to the café she had spotted earlier. She parked in front and walked into the restaurant with the newspaper in hand. Soft bells jingled over the door and announced her entrance to the nearly empty dining room.

"Be right with ya. Take a seat wherever you like." The feminine voice called out from the rear of the room, but Charlotte couldn't see the source. She sat in a booth facing the back of the restaurant. The day's specials decorated a chalkboard behind the counter lined with classic barstools. A laminated menu was tucked between the salt and pepper shakers on the table. Charlotte glanced at it as the waitress sauntered over. She was young, about Charlotte's own age. A hot pink apron covered her jeans and t-shirt and her name tag read "Chrissy".

"Can I get you something to drink, hon?"

"I'll just have a coffee." Charlotte said. It was two in the afternoon and she wasn't supposed to drink coffee, according to her therapist. *I came out here, didn't I? We'll call it a compromise.* Another concept she was working on. She grabbed the menu and skimmed it.

A moment later, Chrissy came back with a glass of ice water and mug of steaming coffee. Her perky soprano voice interrupted Charlotte's musings. "Anything to eat?"

Charlotte tried to remember how long it had been since she had eaten, but nothing came to mind. "I'll have the club sandwich, no mayo."

Chrissy nodded. "Coming right up." When Chrissy made it back to the counter, she called through the window to the kitchen. "Dad, club sandwich, no mayo!"

Charlotte settled in with her coffee and scanned the newspaper, if you could call it that. She saw an article about tables and chairs for rent from town hall and the upcoming Baptist/Catholic annual softball game. There was one section on 'Finance', which was an editorial on the property values dropping near the railroad tracks. Sports took up the center two pages: an article bemoaning the lack of success of Indiana football, one highlighting the same at Purdue, a summary of Major League Baseball scores, and an in-depth update on the NASCAR standings. The last page was what she wanted, but before she could read it, Chrissy came back with her sandwich.

She set mayo and ketchup on the table and a generous stack of napkins. "Anything else I can get you?"

Charlotte gave a polite smile to the young waitress. "Do you have a pen and paper, by chance?"

Chrissy brightened at the interaction. "Sure thing."

As Charlotte studied her sandwich and thought about the best way to tackle the three-inch-thick monster, she grabbed a french fry. She decided to just go for it and removed the toothpick that was holding it together. She took a bite just as Chrissy returned.

"You new in town or somethin'?" It wasn't an unfriendly question, just more small-town curiosity from what Charlotte could tell.

She choked on her sandwich and struggled to swallow. Coughing, she looked up. "I suppose I am."

Chrissy pushed out her chin. "Huh. We don't get too many new faces in Minden. Everybody trying to get out of here, mostly." Charlotte detected a hint of sadness in the young woman. Maybe she wanted to get out, too, Charlotte considered.

Charlotte offered nothing to that, and the waitress shrugged. "Let me know if you need something. My name's Chrissy. It's a real nice place to live, if you ask me."

"Thanks. I'm Charlotte."

Chrissy gave a broad smile. "Well then, welcome to Minden, Charlotte!"

Charlotte watched her walk away and turned back to the paper. The back page had a half-page ad about a sale at the hardware store and the Classifieds.

Farm north of Minden 2.5 miles, looking for seasonal help. Truck for sale. Tractor for sale. Fresh eggs for sale. Charlotte started to lose hope but kept reading. Puppies, free to a good home. *Hmm, maybe I should get a puppy. Who am I kidding? I can't even feed myself. How am I going to manage to feed something else?* She got to the final listing: "Two bedroom cabin for rent. Contact Ms. Ruth."

No phone number, no address. *Great. This old lady doesn't even know how to put an ad in the paper. There is no way this cabin is livable.* She contemplated how to proceed with the lack of available information.

A bang sounded from the bar as Chrissy set down a stack of plates. Charlotte spoke across the mostly empty restaurant. "Chrissy, do you know Miss Ruth?"

Chrissy spoke loudly as she made her way to Charlotte's table. "Well sure! Everybody knows Miss Ruth. You thinking about renting her cabin?"

Charlotte gave a light shrug. "Maybe. But she didn't list a phone number on her ad, how do I contact her?"

Chrissy waved a hand. "Oh, Miss Ruth doesn't answer her phone anyway. She says people wouldn't stop by and see her if they could call her on the phone instead."

Great, this just gets better and better. "Okay, can I get directions, then?"

"I'm headed over there after I eat, I can take you," a male voice said from the front of the café.

Charlotte jumped at the big voice. She hadn't even noticed him. He was a big guy, with a plaid button down on and a baseball hat covering a thick head of dark hair. Charlotte's city instincts kicked in.

"No thanks, I'd rather drive myself..." *than get kidnapped and murdered in the woods by you,* she finished in her head.

The bearded man conceded with an eyebrow raise. "Alright. I'll lead the way, and you can follow."

Charlotte paused. "Okay, thank you, ..." she looked at him expectantly.

"Todd." He supplied. "Todd Flynn."

"Charlotte." She answered. "Nice to meet you."

"Likewise, ma'am." Then he turned to his coffee and away from her.

Good grief. No one had ever called her ma'am. Well, maybe a bell boy or a secretary trying to explain away a mistake. Chrissy wandered from Charlotte's table over to Todd's and Charlotte eavesdropped.

"While you are there, Todd, make sure you tell Miss Ruth that she is overdue for a visit. I've got a slice of lemon meringue with her name on it," smiled Chrissy.

Todd's smile broadened behind his beard. "I'll tell her, as long as you've got one back there with mine on it."

"Oh shoot, I think I gave yours away," Chrissy said slyly.

"You wouldn't have... You know I come in here every day just for that pie."

They were flirting. Interesting, Charlotte considered as she tuned them out.

Luke Brand parked his hunter green truck back in front of the small office building where he managed his landscaping business. Mulched flower beds and stacked stone features decorated the outside of the small building. A splash of mud fell from the wheel well when he slammed the door. It had already been a long morning; one of his workers got their lawn mower stuck, trying to cut the grass in a low-lying ditch when it was too wet. He had to take his own truck to pull them out, calling him away from another project.

He pulled the baseball cap off and wiped his forehead with a bare arm before replacing it. Then, Luke opened the door to the office and stepped into the air conditioning. The front room acted as a conference room for consultations with clients, although most meetings took place while strolling through a yard or construction site. Past the oval table was the door to his personal office, and Luke moved toward it, his heavy steps loud on the wood floor.

Sometimes, Luke wondered in the realization that he owned his own business. Ten years ago, driving nails into shingles under the beating sun, it would have been beyond even his wildest dreams. Then, he'd been a struggling teenager, kicked out of his own home and with few prospects of a better life. Praise God, he'd avoided the common pitfalls of those in his situation. Drugs, alcohol; none of it had held appeal for him. Only the drive to survive. Even now, he could look back and see how God was orchestrating everything. What God was accomplishing in taking Rachel, he didn't know. When Luke thought about it too long, the ever-present anger flared. As usual, he stuffed it down and focused at the task at hand. Far easier to focus on work, or Ruth, or his endless project of fixing up the cabin he and Rachel had lived in.

It was equally painful and wonderful to work in the space he once shared with his young bride. Her laughter still echoed in the sparsely furnished rooms if he listened closely. *Maybe I should go there this afternoon. I can make a list of things left to finish. And I've got those fixtures to install.* He needed to talk with Ruth anyway. She'd placed the ad for a tenant in the paper again, despite his protests. Just yesterday, Pastor Justin had asked him about it while Luke was trimming the bushes around the church.

Luke moved out of the cabin after Rachel died, unable to live inundated with the memories. Even though he no longer lived at the cabin, Luke couldn't bear to let someone else move in. To do so felt too much like moving on. And how could he move on from Rachel? His guiding light? She'd rescued him all those years before and they'd been so happy. It was perpetual newlywed bliss, his memories insisted. A future just beginning to take shape, ripped from him in a moment.

Luke stepped into his office and ignored the touches of Rachel in the small space. When he'd purchased the small office building and surrounding lots for the fledgling Brand New Landscaping, Rachel had decorated the space. He'd left everything, unable to remove even the feminine curtains he'd immediately ribbed Rachel about choosing. It had been two years since she died. While the sharp, breathtaking pain of the immediate aftermath had subsided, it had only been replaced with a strong, dull ache that never lessened. A constant painful emptiness left where Rachel had been. He was trying to find solace in God, like Ruth did. But every day was a struggle to believe in God's greater plan. At least today, he had the distraction of work. One last glance at maroon, plaid curtains and Luke dove into the pile of invoices he needed to enter in the computer, shutting out the memories and the doubt.

TODD DROVE a black truck with all the bells and whistles. *It looks like it belongs in a monster truck rally,* Charlotte mused, as if she knew what a monster truck rally looked like. Unlike any of the decked out trucks she had seen in St. Louis, this one had been well-used. There were dents and scratches and a good coat of dust covering the whole thing.

Charlotte unlocked her Mazda and Todd laughed. Annoyed, she bit back a glare. "Something wrong?"

"I just hope it has dried out, or you'll never get that little car to Miss Ruth's house." Todd's tone rang with truth, despite the laughter veiled behind it.

Charlotte considered and cringed at the thought

of driving her beloved Mazda on a muddy road. "Well, what should I do?"

"Just let me drive you." He smiled at her. "Please? There is no way I'll get stuck, but..." He looked back at her sporty car.

He certainly looked harmless enough, and his smile was warm and genuine behind his beard. She saw no hint of malice or indication of hidden motive. "Oh alright, but just this once."

Todd walked around, opened the passenger door for her, and helped her climb the three feet into the cab. Charlotte was taken aback at the show of chivalry and considered refusing his assistance. Until she saw the height of the truck floor and considered how she would get her 5'3" frame that high.

They ambled along Main Street back toward the gas station and headed out of town. "Just how far out does Miss Ruth live?"

"Oh, not too far. She's too stubborn to move into town, and too attached to live too far away." They chatted as they proceeded down a county road and then turned on a gravel path. Charlotte gazed at the fields, already harvested – presenting a sepia landscape, surprisingly peaceful.

"So what brings you to Minden?" Todd did nothing to disguise his curiosity.

"I just needed a change of pace," Charlotte replied, but didn't offer anything further. She was too busy admiring the trees. Now that they had passed the empty fields, a thick swash of trees stood on either side of the road. The other side of town had been all empty, flat farmland. But this? This looked like what she could remember of living in Southern Missouri. Whenever she thought of home, she thought of the trees. The rest was too painful to remember.

They pulled off the gravel onto a dirt road. Charlotte was immediately glad that she had agreed to ride with Todd. The road was rutted and still muddy from the last rain. Her little Mazda would have never survived the trip. *I guess I could buy a new car.*

But Charlotte loved her little car.

She loved driving it down the interstate and whipping into her executive parking space. *I guess that's not an option here, anyway.* Charlotte sucked in a breath and told herself to grow up. *It's just a car, Charlie.*

The trees fell away on both sides to reveal a wide front yard in front of the most perfect house Charlotte had ever seen. The house was a deep blue with white trim and a wrap-around porch. But it wasn't actually the house that took her breath away. The yard was beautifully landscaped, with gardens filled with greenery and purple shrubs, potted mums and other fall flowers that Charlotte didn't even recognize. The top leaves of smaller trees scattered throughout were just beginning to change colors from green to reds and yellows. Everything was neatly trimmed, and narrow walking paths wandered through the front and disappeared into the back, where Charlotte could see more gardens. There was a simple white birdbath and several small benches scattered throughout. "Wow," she breathed.

"Sure is somethin', isn't it?" Todd smiled.

Charlotte just nodded as she tried to take in every detail. Todd parked the truck and started to get out. He looked at Charlotte, who was suddenly very nervous. Miss Ruth obviously liked things perfect, and Charlotte was far from that. *Oh, get over it, Charlie. You aren't part of the family, you're just a tenant. I wonder what this 'cabin' looks like.* She pictured a tiny shack with dingy windows and a wood fireplace, and she stifled a laugh at the thought of herself carrying firewood and struggling to light a match. She climbed—or more accurately, jumped— down from the truck and followed Todd toward the house.

The front door swung open and a woman who

Charlotte assumed was the famous Miss Ruth came out. She was younger than Charlotte expected, maybe in her mid-50s. Ruth wore jeans and a flowery blouse, partially covered by a simple black apron she was removing as she walked out. Her fiery red hair popped in the sunlight and Charlotte raised her eyebrows at the unexpected personality. "Todd, my favorite hooligan! What brings you to my door this afternoon?" Ruth's greeting was cheery and vibrant; already a stark contrast to Charlotte's default demeanor.

"Just wanted to see the most beautiful woman in Lincoln County." Todd hugged her and kissed her cheek.

"Oh, you charming boy. Who is this lovely young lady? Are you finally going to give up this bachelor life you lead and settle down?" She winked at Charlotte, who blushed.

Instead of letting Todd answer, Charlotte stepped up and held out her hand. "I'm Charlotte Walters, ma'am. I've been told you have a cabin for rent." She felt awkward. Suit and tie lawyers at a mahogany conference table were no problem, but this motherly figure had Charlotte walking on eggshells. Charlotte didn't know how to imitate the warm, friendly feeling that was pouring out of Ruth, and she defaulted to her interview persona. Cool, calm, collected, and entirely impersonal.

Ruth gave a wide smile.

"I sure do. Very nice to meet you, Charlotte. Please, call me Ruth. Why don't you come on in and we can talk about that cabin. Todd?"

Todd gestured to a metal building down the hill. "I just wanted to grab some tools from the shop, I'll come up and get Charlotte when I'm done."

Charlotte and Miss Ruth walked inside. Charlotte expected an interior as pristine as the exterior, and she was not disappointed. Rich, dark hardwood floors spread from the front door through the entire house. A gorgeous banister decorated the stairs leading to the second floor, and an antique chandelier was the focal piece of the foyer. To the left, French doors led into a formal sitting room, and to the right appeared to be the dining room. Ruth passed both and continued into the kitchen.

"Oh, we came at a bad time." Charlotte apologized as she surveyed the kitchen, which was scattered with mixing bowls and cookie sheets.

"Oh nonsense," Ruth slipped her apron back on, "I'm just whipping up some goodies for the church picnic. We have it every year, and there would be an uprising if I didn't bring enough cookies for everyone." She laughed and gestured at a barstool at the island. "Please have a seat. Tell me about yourself, Charlotte."

"Well, I just moved here, I guess you could say, from St. Louis. I'm very responsible and have never missed a payment on anything." Charlotte resisted the urge to squirm.

Ruth waved a hand, "Oh, that's not what I meant, dear. Tell me where you grew up, why you are here in Minden. What do you do for fun?" Ruth began measuring something from a white canister.

Fun? Charlotte decided to ignore that one and start at the beginning, leaving out most of the details. For Ruth's sake. And her own. "Oh, I grew up in Southern Missouri with my parents and two sisters." She rarely thought of her family any more, and skipped over to where she felt like her life really began. "I left for college at seventeen. I moved to St. Louis and have lived there ever since. Then," Charlotte paused, reconsidered, "I decided I needed a change of pace." That seemed safe.

Ruth listened and continued to mix a batch of cookie dough. "I see. Well, I can certainly understand that."

Charlotte almost sighed with relief. The last

thing she wanted to do was explain all the gory details of her fall from glory.

Ruth handed her a spoon with some cookie dough on it. "What do you think?"

Charlotte took the spoon and had a flashback to being five years old and licking the batter off the beaters at her grandmother's house. She tasted the cookie dough and closed her eyes. "It's delicious. What kind of cookies are these?" She'd never had anything like them. They had peanut butter and chocolate chips, but also oatmeal and M&Ms. It was like a combination of every type of cookie Charlotte had ever had.

"I call them 'Kitchen Sink' cookies, since they have a little of everything in them."

Charlotte nodded, "That's fitting."

Ruth laughed and nodded. She gestured at the timer that just went off, "Just let me get this batch out of the oven and we can go take a look at the cabin."

3

The cabin was tucked in the trees on the edge of the property. They walked down a small wooden staircase and into the opening for the cabin. It wasn't what Charlotte had envisioned at all. In fact, she thought calling it a cabin was fundamentally incorrect. *It's a cottage,* she realized with a grin. "It's lovely, Ruth." And it was. Stylistically, it imitated the main house, with a small front porch. It was painted white, with dark blue shutters and trim. There were even a few rose bushes lining the front walk, which led to a private driveway. The main house and driveway was barely visible through the trees

"I'm glad you think so. My son, Luke, fixed it up for me so I could rent it out."

Charlotte grimaced, realizing that she had been so self-absorbed that she hadn't even asked Miss Ruth anything about herself. "That's really nice of him; does your family live around here?"

Charlotte noticed a slight dimming of Ruth's smile, "He's in Minden now." Ruth walked to the front and opened the door, it was unlocked. *Small towns*, Charlotte realized.

Inside, the cottage was nothing special, but it was clean. There were a couple pieces of furniture – a small table with two chairs, a couch and a club chair. The kitchen was modern, but not flashy. The hardwoods were similar to the main house, also. Charlotte wandered through the rooms, imagining the possibilities. She was mentally choosing window treatments and bedding and then chided herself. *You don't even know if it's yours, yet.*

She held out her arms and spun back toward Ruth, standing in the entry. "I love it, Ruth. What do you need from me?"

Ruth clapped her hands together. "Oh, I'm so glad. Rent will be $400/month, and that includes utilities since they are hooked up to the main house. How long will you be staying?"

The words jumped out of her mouth. "One year." *Am I staying a year? Why did I say that?* She hadn't come with a timeline in mind, but it spilled out when she went to answer Ruth's question. *I guess I'll be here longer than I thought.*

"Very well. It's yours."

Charlotte stared. "Are you sure? No references, no credit check?"

"Oh honey, you aren't in the city any more. You seem trustworthy, and I'll give you the benefit of the doubt." Ruth smiled, "unless, of course – there is something you'd like to tell me?"

"No, no, nothing like that. Just surprised I guess."

"Well, I'll leave you here to look around some more. I need to go put some more cookies in the oven." Ruth turned at walked back to the main house. She paused at the door and looked back. "I'm glad you are here, Charlotte. I have a feeling this is going to be exactly what you need." Then, leaving Charlotte with a confused smile behind, Ruth made her way out the door.

Charlotte looked around and for the first time in what seemed like months, she smiled to herself. *This is better than I could have planned.* She briefly considered spinning in circles, and then heard an engine outside. She looked out the window and saw a familiar-looking green, albeit mud-covered, truck pulling up the cabin's narrow drive.

As HE PULLED up to the cabin, Luke smiled tightly. The cabin always had that effect on him. It was, after all, full of so many bittersweet memories. He got out of the cab and grabbed the things he had gotten at the hardware store sale and his toolbox. *It's about time I got those fixtures replaced. Not to mention the locks on the door.* He headed up the porch and froze as he got to the front door. He heard someone walking inside, and the door swung open.

Luke's first instinct was to attack first, ask questions later, but he restrained himself as he saw the woman standing before him. Luke hadn't noticed earlier at the gas station, but she was stunning. Her face was angular and intense and pinched in a scowl so severe he couldn't imagine what it would look like if she ever deigned to smile at him. She'd be gorgeous if she smiled. She was several inches shorter than him, although he was only 5' 8". Her light-blonde hair tumbled over her shoulders in big bouncy curls, but what caught his attention were her eyes. They were a pale green, suited to her ivory skin and light sprinkle of freckles. Those eyes narrowed and he realized she had spoken to him. "Pardon?" Luke asked, his voice catching in his throat.

"I said, can I help you?" She was clearly irritated.

Luke recoiled. "Me? No. But you can tell me what you are doing here. This is private property." After the initial shock and the realization that she wasn't a physical threat, Luke began to think this well-dressed woman posed a very different kind of threat. This was wrong; this felt wrong. This place was his. Well, technically, it was Ruth's but it might as well be his. This woman didn't belong here, that much was obvious from silky top and jeans she had on. They had a crease, for crying out loud. *Who has jeans with a crease down the front?*

"I'm the new tenant. And you are?" Skepticism filled her voice, along with a fair dose of condescension.

"Oh." Luke faltered. A tenant? Ruth hadn't been able to rent out the cabin despite almost a year of trying. Of course, he'd been secretly discouraging any potential renters. He wouldn't admit it to Ruth, but he just wasn't ready to see anyone else living here. Instead he kept working on it, making small improvements, and claiming it wasn't ready. "Uh, I'm Luke. I'm Ruth's..." he cut himself off and then continued. "She should have told me she had rented it out," he finished lamely.

"Well, I'm sure she would have gotten around to it. We just figured it out ourselves ten minutes ago."

Of course you did. You move fast, don't you? "And you are?" He was being rude and couldn't help it. *She shouldn't be here. No one should be here!*

"I'm Charlotte." Her green eyes studied him intently, making him a bit uncomfortable. She added nothing more to her introduction.

"Well, Charlotte, I think you and I ought to go have a talk with Mom." *And I think I need to find a way to talk her out of this.* Luke turned away and headed up the path to the main house, practically stomping.

Watching him storm away, she couldn't believe the nerve of this guy. Afterall, she had an agreement with Ruth and that was all that mattered. But then, she began to doubt the strong position she'd just portrayed. Surely Ruth would side with her son and decide not to rent to her after all.

After he stormed off toward the main house, she looked back into the cottage, sighed, and pulled the door closed behind her. A few moments ago, Charlotte had been mentally picking out throw pillows, and now she wondered if she even had a place to stay tonight. No matter how much Charlotte wanted to stay, Luke definitely had more pull with Ruth than she did. Charlotte didn't doubt that he would use every bit of that pull to get her out of the cottage after what she saw in his eyes and body language.

She wasn't disappointed. Charlotte strolled into the kitchen about a minute after Luke, but hung in the doorway, out of sight. Luke was pleading with Ruth as she put a batch of cookies in the oven. "It's not ready yet, Mom. I was coming even today to work on things! The light fixtures need replaced and there is no way that furnace will make it through winter."

Ruth nodded, as though she agreed, but she handed him a cookie and smiled. "Well, then I guess it is a good thing it is still September, and a warm one at that. I'm sure Charlotte won't mind having you intrude one weekend to fix the furnace."

Luke wasn't ready to give up, Charlotte could see that. He started to argue again, but Ruth cut him off. "Now, Charlotte needs a place to stay and I have a place to give her. I'm tired of living out here alone and this young lady has done nothing to deserve being thrown out before she's even moved in. I know you've been chasing out renters and trying to pretend that lovely little house is a monument. I'm putting my foot down, young man."

Luke hung his head. Charlotte bit back a smile. He looked so much like a rebuked child. She had mistaken him for a teenager at the gas station earlier, although now she could see that had been an assumption on her part based on the jeans and ball cap. *What kind of grown man walks around in a baseball cap? At least he cleaned up the muddy boots before coming here.* Ruth continued, softer now, "I need this. Charlotte needs this. And believe it or not, so do you." Ruth grabbed his shoulders and kissed his forehead. Charlotte recognized the love between the two of them, and it made her ache. When was the last time someone comforted her and kissed her hairline? She shrugged off the thought and walked into the kitchen.

Hearing her, Luke straightened and Ruth smiled, "Perfect timing, child. I heard you already met Lucas. I was just telling him how much I was looking forward to having you as a tenant."

"I'm looking forward to it, too." She glanced at Luke. He seemed to have relaxed some, but he wasn't looking at her. Instead, he stared at the cookie still uneaten in his hand. He looked up at her and met her stare. Charlotte thought the look in his eyes might be anger or stubbornness. As he studied her, she noticed his eyes dilate and immediately read the signal as desire. *Nope, definitely not that last one, he doesn't want me anywhere near him! Get a grip, Charlie,* she chided. *You must be rustier at reading people than you thought.* She wasn't here to get involved anyway. Just a little R&R in a sleepy little town. Then, she'd go rebuild her career. It was the most important thing she had. And one year here wouldn't change that.

TODD GAVE Charlotte a ride back to town, but not before Luke impolitely brushed off Ruth's suggestion that he take her back instead. Ruth thought it would give them a chance to "get to know each other". Luke mumbled some sort of excuse before kissing Ruth on the cheek and rushing out the door. Todd looked as baffled as Charlotte felt, but joked about it good-naturedly on the way back. Now, she sat in his truck as they pulled up to her Mazda. *Drat, forgot about that one little detail, didn't you? It would probably help if you could actually make it up the road to your house, smart one.* Charlotte sighed and Todd laughed. "Guess we will have to find you a new ride, right?" He kept driving past the Mazda and turned left a few blocks later. They headed south out of town, and he stopped at a sketchy-looking building with three garage doors and countless cars and trucks out front with dented fenders or one wheel missing.

Charlotte looked at Todd skeptically. "No."

Todd tipped his head toward her. "Now, now. Roy's got the best service and the best deals in a hundred miles." Todd's voice was patient, but firm.

"Absolutely not." Her Mazda was purchased for full price in a gleaming showroom on the northside of St. Louis. There was no possible way she was going to find anything she liked in the pile of junky cars.

"Give it a chance." Todd looked at her with adorable brown puppy dog eyes. "If you don't find something you like, I'll buy you a drink to make it up to you."

A drink did sound tempting, along with the unspoken offer of friendship. Charlotte liked Todd and the idea of seeing him again Having a friend here would make the year go faster. "It's a deal." She shot him one last glance before she jumped down, "Besides, there is absolutely zero chance I will find something on this lot."

He laughed and climbed out, "If you say so."

As they walked, Todd explained how it worked. Roy didn't fix anything until he knew he had a buyer. He did show them the truck he was finishing up for someone else. Charlotte had to admit, it looked good. She talked herself into keeping an open mind and started around the lot. Roy went along, pointing out cars and trucks he thought might work. Todd explained that she was moving into Ruth's cabin, which drew barks of laughter when he told Roy about her current set of wheels. "What you need is something reliable. Something with 4-wheel drive, and something you can get a little mud on. This here is a really nice little Ranger pick-up. Manual transmission, 4-wheel drive."

Charlotte cut him off, "Sorry, I can't drive a stick. It'll have to be an automatic."

Roy whistled, "Wooo-eee, we sure do got a city girl here. Alright alright, I'll make sure it's an automatic for ya." He looked up and to the left, thinking. "I got it." Roy walked further away from the main building and cut across two rows of cars, stopping next to a dark blue Jeep Liberty. He put his hand on it. "This is perfect for you. It's compact, durable, and will handle anything Ruth's driveway can throw at it. Just needs a gasket replaced, a new battery, and some new tires."

Charlotte looked it over, it didn't look as rough as many of the other vehicles on the lot. In fact, it was kind of great. It wasn't a recent model, but it had held up well. She opened the door, which was unlocked and sat inside. Putting her hands on the wheel, Charlotte looked around, and felt tall. This was a totally different feeling that sitting in her low-riding sports car and she liked it. She grinned and then looked at Todd, who was laughing. "Guess I don't have to buy you that drink after all."

"Nope, looks like I'll owe you one!"

Todd looked to Roy, "How much to get it up and running?"

Roy chewed on the toothpick that had been bouncing from one side of his mouth to the other since they arrived. "Oh...Repairs will be around five, with another five for tires. I'll give you the whole thing for four grand."

Todd scoffed, getting into the negotiation now. "Roy, just because Charlotte is new in town doesn't mean you can pull one over on her. There's no way that is worth a penny over $2800, and you know it." Charlotte bit her tongue, watching the negotiation.

Roy looked pained. "$3600."

Todd looked at Charlotte, who just nodded for him to continue. "$3000. Final offer." Todd stuck out his hand, and Roy grabbed it after a long moment of contemplation. "Deal. But I'm not happy about it." Despite this proclamation, Charlotte could see that the deal was a good one for Roy too. His jaw was relaxed and his eyes remained light and friendly.

"When will it be ready?" Charlotte asked as she got out of her new car.

"I'll have it running by tomorrow afternoon, but I'll have to wait a couple days for the tires. You can take it tomorrow and bring it back for the tires." Roy shook her hand, too. "Nice to meet you, Miss Charlotte."

"Pleasure's all mine, Roy." Charlotte bit her lip to keep the grin from spreading too wide. $3000 for a new car? *This place is further away from the city than I thought.*

Charlotte was still grinning when Todd drove her back to her car. "I can't believe we found something. I can't believe you went down to $3000, I would have paid $3600!"

"Yeah, well, it's a good thing you stayed quiet, then!"

Charlotte threw her head back and laughed. It felt good. Honestly, she couldn't remember the last time she had felt this carefree. "I should probably learn to do that more often."

Todd gave her a look and said "Most women could." He winked at her to let her know he was only kidding. "Where to now, Lottie?"

"Ugh, not a chance. It's Charlotte, or Charlie - if you must."

"Charlie..." Todd studied her face and glanced at her clothes, "you don't really look like a Charlie."

Charlotte shrugged. No one had called her Charlie since she was a kid. Charlie was an all-but-forgotten carefree child, from before everything spiraled out of control with her parents. But it felt kind of right here. "Maybe once I'm driving my new Jeep it'll fit better."

4

Charlotte spent the next few days settling in to her new cottage. She went to Terre Haute one day and bought everything she thought she would need. She was surprised to find sheets at Walmart with a suitable thread count and even bath towels that weren't scratchy. The kitchen in the cottage was sparsely equippes, but since she didn't cook anyway, she wasn't too concerned with the lack of dishes or pots and pans. A set of plastic plates and cups that looked like summer picnic-ware caught her eye. *One dollar for four plates? No way anyone is making money on these.* With a shrug, she placed them in her cart, grabbing all four different colors. She even bought curtains for the front window, the sheer creamy white ones she had imagined blowing in the breeze when she first stood in the cottage.

Charlotte switched cars in town, transferring all her purchases into the Jeep since she had driven her Mazda to the city. *Good lord, am I already thinking of Terre Haute, Indiana as the **city**??!* She grinned at the thought of what her friends would say if they heard that. To them, even St. Louis was on the small side.

Roy kept his end of the bargain, and the Jeep was purring as she headed out of town. She picked up dinner from Chrissy at Bud and Janine's on her way and the smell wafted through the car. Her first Saturday night in Minden. *What do people do around here?* She heard all about the 'big softball game' being held next weekend, but nothing about this Saturday night. *Guess I should have bought a book when I was in town,* she thought. *Not that I would even know what to get. What do I even like to read?* It had been so long since Charlotte had taken the time to read for pure pleasure. Books on personal development and psychology weren't exactly relaxing.

Even when she read the papers, it was more to scout out companies potentially requiring new talent due to misfortune or mismanagement. *It always comes down to one or the other.* Charlotte firmly believed almost any company could succeed if it was managed well and granted a bit of luck. Usually it only took one to get by, but to really succeed - a company needed both. From her former role, Charlotte knew the history of nearly every Fortune 500 company, and not the glossy story printed up in marketing brochures. She heard of the backroom deals—the favors granted from daddy's golfing buddies; as well as the sex, blackmail, and deception that almost always followed those amounts of money. For a long time, she had enjoyed it—even reveled in it. Charlotte excelled at reading people and finding out their secrets. She also excelled at keeping her own. More than once, she had been offered the very job she was interviewing someone for. Charlotte smirked, *I doubt that is going to happen anymore. Not after the way I screwed up. Chalk this one up to mismanagement, plus a little competitor interference.*

With that thought lingering, she pulled into the drive of the cottage. Charlotte smiled, as she did every time she saw the pretty white building tucked in the trees. *Forget about it, Charlie. You are a million miles away from that world now.* She took a deep breath and started carrying her things inside.

LUKE STOOD in the trees and watched her. He was heading to the cabin from the main house. In town earlier, Ruth told him that Charlotte was gone for the day. He'd been hoping she wouldn't find her way back, maybe finding Terre Haute more her speed. *So much for dreams coming true.* Luke watched her carry in big bags with what looked to be a thousand pillows in them. *I will never understand women. This cabin doesn't need frills.* In fact, he had thrown out all the curtains and pillows one night when he couldn't bear to look at them any longer. The cabin had been bare ever since. Charlotte struggled with a box of ready to assemble furniture, a desk of some sort. *What could she possibly need a desk for? She probably thinks she is going to pen the next great American novel or something.* Luke rolled his eyes. He ignored his prickling conscience, nudging him to offer to help, Luke turned back and forced himself to stop wondering about this mysterious creature invading his world. He would replace the fixtures another time. After Miss Walters was gone. She couldn't stick around long.

Instead of going back to the main house like he knew he should, he went back to his truck and started it up. He jabbed at the power button to silence the radio and clenched his jaw. He knew Ruth was going to be disappointed he didn't stop by like he'd mentioned, but he figured he wouldn't be very good company tonight. Ruth would be all understanding and sympathetic about his attitude toward Charlotte, but then she'd box his ears and make him straighten up. He wasn't quite ready for that yet.

Luke drove through town and picked up a couple of slices of pizza from the warmer at the QuikStop. He tried not to think about what he could have eaten at Ruth's instead as he ate the cardboard pizza in his truck. His house was tucked on the other side of town, a couple of streets off Main. It was a small, two-bedroom house with a yard the size of a postage-stamp. Luke always made sure the landscaping was nice. Landscaping was his job and people knew which house was his. Luke figured it better look like he was capable of keeping grass alive and bushes trimmed. Other than that, the house was basic. Perfect for a bachelor, he admitted. As he walked inside, he thought—not for the first time—*Rachel would have hated this house.* The beige walls, beige carpet, beige everything would have had her driving to Terre Haute to buy pillows and throw blankets. And probably some paint.

Sometimes, Luke enjoyed this quiet, cozy house. He relished in the fact that it was his and that he'd earned every square foot of it. He turned the music up too loud or ate ice cream for breakfast just because he could. Other times, like tonight—the coziness just felt like claustrophobia and the quiet just felt like emptiness. Luke thought about the years he lived in the cabin with Rachel. The cabin, surrounded by woods was always, and yet never, quiet. It was peaceful, though. The sound of Rachel humming in the kitchen, the birds in the morning, or the cicadas at night. The space was constantly filled with laughter. That was what he missed most. Luke didn't think this new, city-slicker business woman was going to add laughter to the cabin. Charlotte didn't look like she'd laughed in years. She was beautiful. But, she was clearly so uptight and stressed he was confident she'd run back to the city in a week, maybe less. That'd be just fine with him. *Yep, I don't mind if I never see her beautiful face again. Or those jeans with a stupid creases in them.*

With that thought, Luke flipped on ESPN and tried to distract himself with a baseball game. It took about thirty seconds for him to make the connection from the Cubs to the Cardinals to St. Louis and back to a certain unwanted tenant in his cabin. He punched the power button and flipped the remote to the other side of the couch, disgusted with himself. Luke wandered around the house, picking up laundry and straightening shelves before deciding he had paced every inch of the 1200-square-foot house more times than he could bear in one night. He grabbed a rootbeer and pulled his camping chair onto the back deck. He sat there silently, listening to the train rolling through town, and drowning himself in bittersweet thoughts of Rachel and the future they would never experience.

RUTH WAS ENJOYING a cup of tea on her front porch, admiring the colorful fall sunset and nearing the end of a lengthy conversation with her Creator. Since Charlotte arrived, thoughts and prayers about her new tenant had filled Ruth's mind. She could see that Charlotte was struggling right now, though she didn't know with what. God had brought Charlotte to her for a reason, and Ruth prayed for guidance and opportunity. Then, Charlotte strolled up. *My, my, but you do work fast sometimes, Father,* Ruth thought. *I said I wanted the opportunity to reach her, I didn't say I was ready tonight! Help me show her You, Lord. Speak through me, the words she needs to hear.*

Ruth smiled and waved a hand toward Charlotte as she crossed the drive. "What a beautiful evening, isn't it?" The sun was just sinking below the tree line and the fireflies could be seen in the shadows. It had cooled off from the moderate heat of the day. But, with a warm, gentle breeze and clear skies, it was everything Ruth had come to love about fall in Indiana.

Charlotte agreed. "It really is. Is it always like this?" The woods came alive with the sounds of the night. Charlotte breathed in deeply, enjoying the fragrance of the moist earth, flowers, and cedar. At Ruth's comment about the changing seasons and the brief window of perfect weather in between them, Charlotte nodded. "Autumn is my favorite. Living in the city, I missed the trees most when I knew the leaves were changing."

"It's my favorite time of year, too. Reminds me that 'there is a time for everything under the sun. A time for living and a time for dying'." Charlotte's forehead wrinkled, as though she thought the sentiment morbid, but it gave Ruth peace. Her life had been filled with both laughter and tears, life and death. Such heartbreaking death; both her husband and her daughter gone far before their time.

Ruth chased the thoughts of loss from her mind and sipped her tea. "What can I do for you tonight, Charlotte?"

Charlotte's insecurity showed as she admitted, "Well, I don't really know if you'd be willing to, but I'd like to ask to borrow a book?"

Ruth felt the buzz of excitement. This was an opportunity! "Of course! You can check out my bookshelf and borrow anything you'd like. What do you like to read; maybe I can suggest something?" She didn't know what she could suggest; Ruth felt the self-imposed pressure to make sure her recommendation was exactly right.

Charlotte frowned. "Well, actually... Oh boy, this feels strange. I don't really know what I like these days." Charlotte's green eyes looked up at Ruth. "It's been a long time since I read anything. I used to like the bestsellers, like the Oprah book club books."

"Okay..." Ruth thought about it before replying, "I don't really buy many of those books—many of them are too far outside my comfort zone, but I do have a couple novels that lean that direction. Follow me." Ruth led her inside and to the formal sitting room.

On the wall backing the front hallway, stood two bookshelves. There were more on the wall across from the window ." Ruth traced the spines with her finger as she skimmed titles. Which one? *Which one, Lord?* Her books were well-loved, some with leather binding, some with dust jackets. Some were worn paperbacks with cracked spines from repeated readings. Finally, an author caught her eye and Ruth smiled to the shelf. She pulled out a short book, relatively new. "Here we go. Richard Paul Evans is one of my favorite authors these days." Charlotte scanned the cover, which boasted the New York Times best-selling author tag and a picture of a snowflake.

"I'll give it a try. Thank you, Ruth."

Ruth smiled, feeling relieved. "Of course. Anything you need, just let me know. Would you like a glass of tea? I was going to sit on the porch for a while longer."

Charlotte hesitated, and then relented to Ruth's sincere gaze. "As long as you're sure I'm not imposing."

"Nonsense," Ruth waved her off. "I'll just go grab the pitcher and a glass. Make yourself comfortable on the porch."

Ruth busied herself getting the tea, and placed a couple cookies on a plate as well. *You are so good,*

Abba. Thank you for leading me to the right book for her. Open her heart to your prompting.

When Ruth returned to the porch, Charlotte was two pages into the prologue of the book. "I really hope you like it, dear. It is one of my favorite stories of all time." Ruth wasn't speaking of this book, in particular, but rather the story it relayed. The book was a modern-day telling of the prodigal son from the book of Luke. The overtones of faith and Christianity were not so obvious as to turn off the average reader, but poignant enough to speak to someone who was already starting to listen.

"With your recommendation, I'm sure it will be just what I'm looking for."

"I sure hope so." They sat in comfortable silence for a few minutes, watching as the last of the red in the western sky faded to pink and then purple. Finally, Ruth broke the silence and asked, "What do you have planned for the rest of the weekend?"

"To be honest, I'm not really sure yet. Does Luke need some time at the cabin? I can find somewhere else to be." Ruth shook her head.

"Oh no, you don't have to accommodate him. There is no reason you can't be there while he is." Luke needed to let go. Charlotte was supposed to be here—healing from whatever had made her run so far from her past.

"Well, I saw him come up to the cottage earlier, but he left when he saw me unloading my car."

Ruth clicked her tongue. "I didn't realize he was here today. Either way, don't you worry about him, dear. He'll come when he's ready." Ruth tucked the information away for later and then changed the subject. "I was wondering if you would like to come to the softball game next weekend? Everyone in town will be there, and it's a great time. It would be a perfect opportunity for you to make friends."

Charlotte's eyes grew wide. Then, she considered. "That sounds great. Right now, I really only know Todd. What time, and where do I go?"

Ruth smiled. She was grateful Todd had befriended Charlotte. "Oh, just meet up here at the main house next Saturday around two and we'll go together."

"Perfect." Charlotte washed down her cookie with her last drink of iced tea. Ruth met her gaze when Charlotte stood. "Thank you. For everything."

Ruth just nodded and looked out toward the darkening woods, rocking back and forth with a contented smile on her face. When you pay attention, it's easy to see God working. Even the smallest interactions serve His good purpose. Ruth was grateful for the conversation with Charlotte. As time went on, she might discover what chased the young woman here from the city. But Ruth had no doubt God brought Charlotte to Minden and to the cabin.

But what was she going to do about Luke? It killed Ruth to see him hurting. He'd been different since Rachel died, though she couldn't really blame him. No man deserved to lose what Luke did that day. But his sorrow was suffocating him. Ruth lifted yet another prayer for her son-in-law. Another plea added to the thousands she'd uttered on his behalf since he came home for Thanksgiving ten years ago. And hundreds in the last year, as she watched him cling to the past instead of to Jesus.

5

Charlotte spent the next couple of days holed up at the cabin. She read the book Ruth lent her, and tried to forget how it made her think about her parents. They definitely wouldn't welcome her home with open arms—not that she would think about going back. She moved the couch to one side of the room so she could do yoga in the middle of the floor but soon grew tired of the silence. Charlotte missed her yoga class with the relaxing music and instructors soothing voice. Trapped in this tiny cottage, however charming; she was going stir crazy. Perhaps coming here was a terrible idea after all.

Every now and then, she saw Luke's truck at the

main house through the trees and she saw him start down the path to the cottage before turning around and walking away. *I guess I wouldn't blame him for avoiding me. I was pretty rude to him that first day. But he was rude to me, too! How could a man like that be Ruth's son?* Charlotte thought about how warm and open Ruth was. Ruth was everything she'd dreamed about having in a mother. Then, she thought about how cold and rigid and unyielding Luke was. It just didn't make sense to her.

After a day or two of wandering around the cabin aimlessly, Charlotte was miserable. How could she not even know how she liked to spend her time? She used to spend her time reading the news and working, with the occasional yoga class thrown in. But, she'd done as much yoga as she could handle. There was no work to do and no newspapers. She didn't even have internet access. In desperation, Charlotte resolved to do something she'd always wanted to do: she was going to bake. The extent of her baking experience to this point was refrigerated cookie dough. Usually, a quarter of the dough never made it to the oven.

Charlotte went to Ruth's and borrowed a cookbook and a cake pan. After assuring Ruth that she didn't need any help, Ruth had given her a bag with measuring cups and spoons, an electric hand mixer, and a look full of skepticism. Looking at the giant bag of kitchen utensils, Charlotte began to doubt her decision. But, she had an entire day ahead of her and nothing else on the horizon, so she flipped through the cookbook. There, on page 253 in the dessert section, she spotted a gorgeous picture of a decadent chocolate cake. She carefully read the ingredients and realized the grocery shopping she had done was clearly not completed with baking in mind. Charlotte carefully transcribed the list of ingredients onto paper for grocery shopping in her neat block handwriting.

Flour
Sugar
Cocoa powder
Baking soda
Baking powder
Buttermilk
Vanilla
Salt
Eggs
Vegetable oil
What exactly is the difference between baking

soda and baking powder? And where do you buy buttermilk? Charlotte ignored the feeling she was in over her head and grabbed her keys, determined to meet the challenge she'd laid out before herself.

There was no full-service grocery store in Minden, and Charlotte was fairly confident they didn't carry things like buttermilk or baking powder at the QuikStop off the highway. She drove the twenty minutes to Greencastle to shop at the Apple-Mart. Ignoring the urge to search for talk radio on the dial, she listened to the country music she was getting more and more familiar with.

Usually, her grocery shopping consisted of produce and the freezer section. She tried to strike a balance between fresh fruits and veggies and the frozen pizzas and Lean Cuisine meals she so often resorted to. It took Charlotte five minutes to find the aisle designated for all things baking. Staring at the approximately fifty types of flour, she considered her options. Baking flour sounded promising, but so did cake flour. And then there was all-purpose flour. Then, there was one that said "unbleached" flour. Did flour have bleach in it? *Gross.* There was bread flour and almond flour, and something called spelt. As she studied the different varieties of flour, she watched other shoppers. They seemed to know what they were getting and all went straight for the "all-purpose" flour. *Okay, let's just go with that. It says it is 'all-purpose', right?*

She picked up baking soda and baking powder, even though they were right next to each other and were probably the same thing. But the recipe called out both of them, and Charlotte always followed the rules. Cocoa powder was in the same aisle too, and she was grateful the recipe had specified 'unsweetened' so she didn't spend another ten minutes looking at all the varieties. Charlotte grabbed sugar, debating shortly between powdered and granulated before decided that 'normal' sugar was probably the one with the most empty space on the shelf in front of it, where other shoppers had removed bags.

Charlotte added vegetable oil and salt to her growing pile in her cart, followed by vanilla extract. All that was left to find was eggs and buttermilk. She went to the coolers at the back of the store and found eggs. She looked at the coolers with gallons of milk, carefully reading each variety before coming to the conclusion that buttermilk wasn't here.

With one last-ditch effort, she flagged down a store employee and asked, "Excuse me; do you sell buttermilk?"

The tall, young man smiled cordially. "Oh sure,

it's right here." He stepped two coolers to the left and pointed to a row of smaller milk containers along with half-and-half, sour cream, and Reddi-whip. The largest container of buttermilk was only thirty-two ounces. Charlotte tried to remember how much she would need for the recipe, but couldn't. She bought two.

After all double checking her list and the inventory of her cart, she went to the front of the store and loaded the items on the belt. Charlotte's eyes bugged at the announced total. Her cake was going to cost over thirty dollars! Although she briefly considered taking it all back and buying a chocolate cake from the bakery at the grocery store, she handed over her credit card and focused on how delicious her chocolate cake was going to be.

Twenty-five minutes later, Charlotte was back at the cottage with her groceries unloaded. She grabbed one of the round cake pans Ruth had given her, wondering for a second why there were two before shrugging it off.

Twice, Charlotte read the recipe from start to finish, and then she began. She preheated the oven and began adding ingredients to the mixing bowl. When she turned the mixer back on after adding the flour and cocoa, a dust cloud erupted. A fine mist of flour coated her and the surrounding three feet of countertop, but she had what tasted to her like a very delicious chocolate cake batter.

Checking the recipe again, she paused at reading "greased cake pan". She didn't have any cooking spray and wasn't sure what to do. Deciding to improvise, Charlotte added some of the vegetable oil to the pan and rubbed it around with a paper towel. Satisfied with her handiwork, she dumped the cake batter into the pan, pleased when it all fit perfectly and filled the pan nearly to the top. After carefully setting the cake in the oven, she set the timer for thirty minutes as directed. Charlotte grabbed a glass of water to wash down the spoonful of batter salvaged from the edges of the bowl. Then, she went out on the porch to wait.

Twenty minutes later, something acrid and smoky assaulted her nose. Worried her cake had somehow cooked super quickly and was beginning to burn, she ran inside. In the cabin, it was worse; the smoke thicker and more noticeable. Turning on the light in the oven, her stomach dropped. Her beautiful round cake pan with delicious chocolate batter was bubbling and overflowing into a gloopy brown mess on the bottom of the oven, slowly turning to char where it touched the heating elements. Defeated, Charlotte sat on the floor, leaning against the oven and tried to choke back the thick, hot feeling in her throat. She pressed the backs of her wrists to her eye-socket pushing back the stinging tears behind her eyes. Another failure in a long line of recent disasters. First, the string of candidate placements with bad results and then, the leaked development document. Suddenly overwhelmed by the reality that, despite years of evidence to the contrary, Charlotte was the screw-up she'd always feared becoming. It was a hereditary trait after all. While the smell of burnt chocolate surrounded her, she thought pitifully, *at least it can't get any worse.*

That thought seemed a cruel joke when the door to the cabin slammed into the wall behind it, despite having already been left open by Charlotte in her haste to rescue her cake. Luke rushed in with wide eyes scanning the room. Charlotte could only bury her head in her hands further. A laugh bubbled up and escaped, unable to be restrained. The first wave weakened the floodgates, and then, Charlotte completely lost control in the absurdity of it.

～

LUKE ASSESSED the cabin quickly and zeroed in on the mess of measuring spoons and open flour and sugar containers. His eyes shifted to the crazy woman sitting in front of a stove emitting smoke and the awful choking scent of something burning. Instead of turning off the oven, he noticed; she was laughing. And not just lightly. Charlotte was laughing hysterically. Loud, full belly laughs with tears streaming down her face. He wasn't an expert, but Luke was pretty sure she was having a nervous breakdown.

Cautiously, as though approaching a wounded animal, he walked toward her and turned off the oven and turned on the vent hood. He sank to the floor and briefly looked in the glass door where the light still illuminated the boiling mud pie that was currently escaping the confines of a cake pan that was far too small. He decided that while it was an absolute mess, the more pressing issue was sitting on the floor beside him, still laughing with great big gasps. Charlotte composed herself, looked at him, and then burst into laughter again.

"Oh my, oh geez." Charlotte struggled to breathe through tears and chuckles that still overtook her every couple of seconds.

"Umm, are you okay?" Still unsure if he could leave her alone, Luke tried to get her talking.

At that, she snorted and laughed again. Luke physically felt his defenses weaken upon hearing her laugh and the most adorable snuffle. "I think so... I just... You. Here. Now. Of course."

"Okay?" Luke didn't know what that meant, but she was slowly becoming more composed. He glanced behind her, "You're going to have to clean that up."

She rolled her eyes at him. "Don't worry. I will." Charlotte wiped her face, tracing under her eyes with a careful finger like women always did to avoid smearing mascara. She blinked at him, as though waiting for something. Luke didn't move, just studied her red-rimmed eyes and smattering of freckles on her impossibly smooth skin. "You can leave now." She looked pointedly toward the door. Now that the heating elements were turned off, the smoke was clearing and the smell was getting better.

Luke nodded and stood up. He held his hand down to her and helped her up out of reflex more than anything else. As soon as she was vertical, he released her hand. Part of him wanted to pull her close and reassure her that her failure was no big deal. The other wanted to run. Far away. Afraid of his conflicted emotions, he sought his escape. Luke looked around, surveying the mess and said with a sardonic tone, "Try not to burn the place down again." With that snide comment hanging in the air and her stunned face etched in his memory, he walked out, mentally smacking himself for essentially kicking a wounded puppy.

Later, Luke laughed out loud at the memory of Charlotte, with her pressed jeans and fancy shirt sitting on the floor in the kitchen of the cabin, covered in flour and laughing maniacally. It was a side of Charlotte he'd never expected to see. She was always so calm, almost cold in her regard of him. He'd started to think that perhaps she never smiled. But, wow – she had been beautiful when she laughed. And he really wanted to make her laugh again.

Of course, the parting shot he'd left when departing the cabin probably didn't win him any points. Luke always struggled with sarcasm and snarkiness – a relic of his days before God; before Rachel. Charlotte seemed to be bringing out the worst in him.

Part of him knew he was being unreasonable. That having Charlotte live in the cabin wasn't the end of the world. And part of him didn't care if he was being cruel or inconsiderate. Yet, after seeing her laugh…. Luke attempted to shake off the memory. Before it drifted away entirely, he laughed again at the thought of wrinkle-free Charlotte scrubbing burnt cake batter out of the bottom of the stove.

6

———

The next time Luke saw Charlotte, he was finally going to swap out the lighting fixtures he had been meaning to. They were sitting in the cab of his truck, mocking his inability to find the courage to go to the cabin when Charlotte might be there. She headed out the door to the cabin when he pulled up, her hair in a ponytail and the first pair of tennis shoes he'd ever seen her wear on her feet.

Luke stuck his head out the window and yelled, "Where are you going?" He sounded harsh, even to himself. *But what was Charlotte thinking?*

"Well, hi to you too. I'm just going to take a little walk in the woods." Her irritation was evident and she attempted to walk away.

Luke called out, "You shouldn't go for a hike alone. And where are your supplies?" He opened the door and stepped out.

Charlotte turned and raised her empty hands in a shrug. "What supplies? I'm not backpacking the Appalachian trail. I'm taking a short walk in the woods. I promise, I'll be fine." Her tone was sarcastic and turned to curious when she asked, "What are you doing here anyway?"

Luke wasn't giving up that easily. He'd gotten lost in these woods himself a time or two. His words came out as a lecture, despite his good intentions. "You at least need to bring some water. And those shorts," *if you could call them shorts, as tiny as they were,* Luke added mentally, "are definitely not what you should be wearing."

Charlotte's eyes widened. "Excuse me? What's wrong with my shorts? Never seen a woman's legs before, Mr. Brand?" She spoke quickly, her voice rising with each question. "Too risqué for you? Maybe you'd like me to put on a snowsuit, or a burka. Then you wouldn't be subject to having to stare at my pasty white legs." Charlotte was fired up now, and when Luke started to speak a response, she promptly turned on her heel and marched off into the woods.

"No, Charlotte – that's not what – arghh!" he muttered. He hadn't been saying she needed to cover her legs because he didn't want to look at them. *Not that I did want to look at them. Nope, I definitely did not want to look at them. Even if they were muscular and smooth...* Luke's thought trailed off, remembering her stomping away in those cute tennis shoes. *And they were pretty pale.* He laughed. But he'd been thinking of the underbrush and the sticks that would be present on the unkempt path. About how she would get thirsty and need water on her hike, even a short one; and how you should always wear long pants hiking so you didn't get chiggers or scratches or poison ivy. Luke shook his head at her stubbornness and carried the light fixtures into the cabin. It was a simple job, and he was done only thirty minutes later. Charlotte wasn't back yet. Knowing she'd need it, he jogged up to the main house and brought back the calamine lotion. Then, somewhat afraid he would have to venture into the woods himself, he waited on the porch until he heard Charlotte returning. Before she entered the clearing, he was gone – rambling in his pickup down the rutted drive.

"STUPID, MISOGYNISTIC, INFURIATING MAN!" Charlotte had been muttering similar descriptions of her landlord's son most of her hike, stopping only to admire a small doe she saw 100 yards ahead and to stand on a fallen log and enjoy the sound of the woods around her. But, most of the trail was overgrown and she was frustrated beyond anything that Luke had been right. She shouldn't have been wearing shorts. "I'm Luke, I know everything. Blah blah blah. Do what I say, Charlotte." She tore her shoelace loose from a vine that entangled it and blew her bangs out of her face with a huff. Finally, she exited the woods into the clearing of the cottage. Her legs were scraped by tiny bushes along the trail and she had found herself slapping at more mosquitoes than she even knew existed. Plus, she was thirsty!

"Condescending, know-it-all, rude son-of-a", the rant died as she entered the cabin and spotted something on her countertop. Ignoring it for now, she got a glass of water and then, deciding she couldn't avoid it forever, she skimmed the note.

Charlotte,

In case you need it.

Luke

Next to the note, Charlotte picked up the small

bottle and tube, Calamine lotion and Neosporin. Firmly ignoring how his thoughtful gesture made her feel, Charlotte gratefully applied the calamine lotion to the dozens of mosquito bites beginning to reveal their welts on her pale legs and arms. Besides, the note practically screamed "I told you so!" without those exact words. *It wasn't nice or sweet. It was cocky and arrogant.* Or so she tried to convince herself.

That evening, Charlotte caved to the desire for a greasy hamburger like the one Todd devoured daily at the café. She grabbed her book, intending to read while she ate like any sane person forced to eat at a restaurant alone. Not that she minded being alone. She'd traveled enough for work and eaten in enough hotel and airport restaurants to know that there were worse things than eating by yourself and not having to share dessert.

The café was busier than when she'd stopped in for lunch, clearly this was the place to be on a Thursday night. She pulled up a seat at the bar and waved to Chrissy who signaled she'd be over in a second. Charlotte looked around behind her to the seated patrons and then rolled her eyes when Luke walked in.

She immediately opened the menu and pretended to be engrossed in its contents, despite knowing exactly what she wanted. Luke sat down as far away from her as possible at the bar, which was only three seats away, but she gave him an A for effort. The only other thing he could have done would have been to take a table meant for four in the main dining area.

Chrissy bounced over, as she seemed to bounce just about everywhere she went. "Hey, Charlotte! I heard you were still in town, I'm so glad!"

Charlotte knew exactly who had been spreading the word of her continued presence, making a mental note to tell Todd that if he wanted to gossip about somebody, he better find a new target because she was boring as an infomercial.

"I'm still here. Should be here for a while, actually. I rented the cottage for a year."

At that admission, she heard Luke snort.

With a raised eyebrow, she turned to the surly man at the end of the bar. "Excuse me? Do you have something to add, Lucas?" Venom in her voice laced his name.

"As a matter of fact I do, Ms. Walters. Honestly, I don't think you'll last a month here, let alone a year." He pointed a finger at her. "You don't belong here. You know it, and I know it. So do whatever it is you need to do, and get out of my cabin."

Charlotte clenched her jaw. *Maybe I don't belong here. But I won't let you scare me away.*

Chrissy gasped. "Lucas Brand, if Miss Ruth heard you treating her guest like that she'd wring your neck."

Charlotte held up a hand. "It's okay Chrissy, I can handle it." Charlotte wasn't intimidated by men like Luke. "He's wrong, anyway. I like it here. As a matter of fact, I had a wonderful hike this afternoon. Which, as it happens – is why I'm starving. Chrissy, I'll take a bacon cheeseburger with extra pickles."

Chrissy looked between the two of them again, and Luke turned back to his menu. Anger radiated from him like the heat from a sunburn. "Curly fries, waffle fries, or steak fries?"

"Waffle fries," Charlotte decided after a brief pause. Sparing one last look along the length of the bar at Luke, she added "and make it to go."

LUKE ATE his dinner at the café in silence, only having to deal with the glares from Chrissy after Charlotte finally left with her food. He figured he was probably pretty lucky Chrissy didn't spit in his mashed potatoes. After he made a jerk of himself at the diner, Luke decided it was time to go see Mom. Thinking of Ruth as 'Mom' always made him briefly think of his birth mom, back in Louisville. While he finished his dinner, he let his mind wander to the sequence of events that had led him to Minden from there so many years ago.

Luke was one month into his job doing landscaping for the grounds crew at Indiana University. He felt lucky, he was pretty sure they thought he was a student when he answered the ad and showed up in the office. So, he hadn't bothered correcting them. Luke needed the money and he didn't know whether being a student was a requirement or not, but he didn't want to risk it. He kept his head down and worked; carrying mulch and raking it out where they told him. He removed perfectly good flowers and planted other perfectly good flowers in their place. The whole process didn't make much sense to him, but he'd do whatever the foreman told him as long as he got paid. It wasn't much, Luke knew that. But housing was cheap around the college town.

An ad on Craigslist said four guys were looking for a fifth roommate. Luke had to share a room, but it would only cost $150 bucks a month. He was pretty sure all the guys thought he was a student too. Luke had just turned eighteen a few days ago. A year before that, his mother had kicked him out because he'd threatened to beat up her boyfriend. After a long line of losers in and out of their house, when Luke found this one stealing from them, he snapped. His mom defended the deadbeat and Luke didn't have anywhere to go. He couch-surfed his friends' houses until Christmas and managed to graduate in December.

Working full-time that spring and summer, Luke saved up money to buy a cheap car and slept in it. He held couple different jobs, but nothing that stuck. Fast food worked as long as he didn't have to deal with customers. Apparently, he wasn't friendly enough. He worked on a roofing crew in Evansville during the summer. A huge hailstorm in the area that April meant tons of work and companies that weren't too picky about the guys they hired. As hot as it was that day mulching flower beds, it didn't come close to the suffocating heat of being on an asphalt roof for ten hours straight. After the demand for replacement roofs died down, he went to Bloomington. One of the guys he roofed with was a student and talked about how cheap it was to live with a group of college students. Access to an apartment and kitchen sounded like heaven compared to sleeping in his car and showering at the truck stop.

When the grounds crew offered him the job doing landscaping for $10/hour, he quickly did the mental math. At forty hours a week, he could make over $1000 a month, even after taxes. It wasn't as much as roofing, but he'd saved quite a bit over the summer and was determined to make it last.

Luke gulped the water and prepared to walk the wheelbarrow filled with the "summer" plants they were replacing back to the trailer, he realized someone was standing in his way. He looked again. Not just someone. An incredibly beautiful someone. She appeared to be talking to him and he hesitantly pulled the earbud from his ear.

"... are just gorgeous, I love the colors. I love Fall weather, but there is just something about the summer flowers that fall blooms can't compare to." She gestured to the wheelbarrow. "What are they going to do with those?"

He struggled to catch up. She'd caught him entirely off-guard. In the month he'd been on campus, he worked on areas all over the expansive grounds. He was pointed at and laughed at, even yelled at by someone who thought he was in their way. Mostly, he was ignored. But no one had talked to him. Not a single one of the privileged students whose parents didn't hate them cared about the lowly landscaper. Why would they? He wasn't part of their world. He just made it beautiful. "Ummm... I'm not sure. I think they keep them in a greenhouse until next summer?"

"Oh that's good. I was worried they just threw them away, ya know?" She smiled at him. Luke felt that smile all the way in his bones. It was warm and bright, and the fact it was directed his way bewildered him. "I'm Rachel." When he didn't respond right away, she looked at him expectantly.

"Oh, uh, yeah. I'm Luke."

"Nice to meet you, Luke. I have to go to class, but I hope I see you around."

Luke couldn't say anything to that as he watched her roll her backpack to the other shoulder and walk away. Her long brown hair was swinging behind her, nearly reaching the bottom of her t-shirt. Luke shook off the encounter and went back to work. As much as he tried not to dwell on the beautiful stranger, her lightly freckled face kept popping into his mind. For the next few days, he kept one eye on the sidewalks when he was working, to no avail. Just when he thought he'd imagined the whole conversation, she showed up. This time, he was weeding a flower bed around a statue of some old guy he didn't recognize.

Her cheery voice cut through the headphones he kept on a lower volume since her first appearance, and he looked up.

"Hi Luke! How's it going?"

Somehow, Luke managed to carry on a conversation with the friendly girl. He found out she was studying Accounting and though he tried to be vague when she asked him his major, he finally revealed that he wasn't a student. Rachel hadn't seemed phased by the news at all. Simply continued chattering about how much she envied that he got to spend all day outside while she had to spend most of it in classrooms or at a computer. The conversation felt all too short to Luke again, but he knew he needed to get back to work.

This pattern continued, Rachel stopping by to talk any time she saw him on campus. Those conversations were the highlight of his weeks. The work didn't seem so dirty, the invisibility to the rest of the students didn't make him so bitter. Instead, he tried to learn new things about the flowers and plants to impress Rachel. He even cut her a flower or two from beds when it worked out that she saw him while he dug out bulbs from lilies or pruned rosebushes that were still miraculously in bloom.

He replayed the conversations again in his mind laying on his air mattress each night. After a month, he finally resolved to ask Rachel to have coffee. He stuttered terribly over the invitation, but his heart soared when she said she'd love to. It was October by then, and coffee lasted hours one Saturday morning as Rachel told funny stories about her hometown. When she finally admitted to a group project meeting she had to go to that afternoon, she invited him to join her for church the next morning.

Luke had never been to church. He contemplated refusing but the opportunity to spend more time with Rachel was irresistible. They started spending a lot of time together. At first, there was nothing romantic. No stolen kisses, no holding hands. Not that he didn't want to, but he still felt like Rachel was so far out of his league, he couldn't bring himself to make a move. There were a couple of girls back in high school, but nothing serious. He'd been too focused on survival and getting out. Luke admired Rachel and the joy and confidence she had. The cynical part of him thought it was because of the easy life she had, when he compared what he knew about her to his own experiences. When she told him how her dad had gotten sick and died when she was ten, he realized he had underestimated her. Rachel made him want to learn more about the God she talked about so easily. She spoke of God in casual conversations, like she was mentioning a friend, not a deity. Rachel insisted that he needed to come back to Minden with her for Thanksgiving. There, he met Miss Ruth, and found a true home for the first time in years.

The thought of Miss Ruth made him smile, as it always did. Shaking himself back to the present, he pulled up to Ruth's house and sighed as he got out of the truck. Luke walked slowly to the main house, and saw his mother-in-law settling in to her customary chair on the front porch with a glass of iced tea and her Bible. *Good to know some things never change,* he thought. She waved him over.

Ruth took one look at him and then sighed, patting the chair beside her. "Have a seat, and tell me about it."

Luke sat, quietly for a minute. "I don't know, Mom. I can't handle seeing her here. It's tearing me up." Ruth waited for more. "The cabin belongs to Rachel. And if we let someone else take it, it's like letting her go all over again." He looked away, ashamed at having admitting the pain he felt.

"Oh, honey," his mother spoke softly. "I know you miss her. But she is a part of you and me, more than she could ever be a part of a building. She would love the idea of someone using this place to start over. You know that as well as I do. And I think Rachel would have loved Charlotte." Luke knew Ruth was right. Rachel was the most caring, tender-hearted person he ever knew. She would have invited Charlotte to stay at the cabin and made Luke sleep alone in the main house if it was what Charlotte needed.

"Probably... She always had a thing for strays. Got that from you, I think." He glanced up at her and gave her a weak smile. "You both took me in when I needed a home and a family. I know I have to let this go. I've been selfish and ugly. I just... It still hurts so much that Rachel isn't here. Instead of being hurt, I turn it into anger. Maybe she is just a convenient target. It's not her fault she is here and Rachel isn't." This was going to be the hardest to admit to Ruth. "I was awful to her at the diner a while ago. I told her she didn't belong and that she should leave." Luke hung his head, ashamed.

"Oh honey. She'll forgive you. And I don't think she's going anywhere. So you're just going to have to get over this." Ruth asked, as she often did, "Have you prayed about it?"

Luke grimaced, "You know I haven't, but that's why you asked." Luke sighed and said, "Thanks Mom."

"Love you, sugar."

"Love you too."

7

When Charlotte walked to the main house on Saturday afternoon, she groaned when she saw Luke's truck in the drive, impossible to mistake - even though it was now a nice, shiny, hunter green. *I cannot catch a break with this guy. Or maybe Ruth is doing it on purpose.*

Luke spotted Charlotte walking up the front steps and opened the door for her. "Hi Ms. Walters. How are you today?"

"Ummm, hi. I'm okay... how are you?" *Besides certifiably bipolar, I guess?* He was wearing athletic shorts and a long sleeved t-shirt along with the same grungy baseball cap she had come to associate with him. *He must be playing in the softball game.*

"I'm very well today, thank you for asking."

Charlotte just raised an eyebrow at him and walked into the house. Thankfully, Ruth was walking down the hallway.

"Perfect timing, Charlotte. We are just about to leave. Would you help me with these?" Ruth was carrying two big Tupperware containers that Charlotte guessed were holding the famed Kitchen Sink Cookies. She took one of the containers and turned back toward the front door, slamming into Luke's shoulder and nearly dropping the cookies. Luke's hand reached out and steadied the container.

"Glad I caught that. Wouldn't want you to be ostracized before anyone even gets a chance to know you."

With his shoulder and chest still pressed lightly against hers, she found it hard to think. "Only delaying the inevitable, I'm sure."

Luke gave her a questioning look, but she gave him a tight smile, grabbed the container and walked past him; letting out a long breath as she bounced down the porch steps.

Why did I say that?? Charlotte mentally kicked herself for getting flustered by the close contact with Luke. *No one here knows you or what you do. Don't ruin it with your big mouth. You would think after ten years, I'd know how to bite my tongue.* The thing was, she did. She'd sat through endless meetings knowing what to say and when to listen; never speaking too soon or without the perfect words. But one accidental brush of Luke's strong frame against hers and she couldn't help but spit out the first words that came to mind.

It had always been hard for Charlotte to make friends. Oh, she got along with people just fine, but eventually she always drove them away. Calling them out on a lie, or digging too far into their personal stories. It was hard for her to trust people. After all, after her parents lied to her a few too many times about where they were going or where they had been she got really good at spotting the lies. She looked at body language, and at tiny muscle movements in a person's face. Where did their eyes go – or even if they didn't give in, where did their eyes want to go. You could see if you looked closely. And Charlotte always looked closely. It was as though she couldn't turn off her interviewing mode. The only friend she'd really had over the last five years or so was Anna. But as soon as Charlotte had stopped interviewing her, and had let her guard down – Anna took everything away from her. She wasn't going to let that happen again. And she certainly didn't care what anyone in this town thought of her; except maybe Ruth.

Luke followed his mother-in-law and Charlotte out of the house, closing the front door behind him, but not bothering to lock it. He'd tried a dozen times to convince Ruth that it wasn't 1968 anymore and she needed to be careful, but she just brushed him off. Her view of the world just simply didn't align with locked doors and security systems. Luke knew she probably didn't even know where the keys to the house were anymore. He had given up that argument long ago. Instead, he just ended up checking on her house every night. It had long become part of his routine to drive to her house and make sure everything was okay. He would lock the door and make sure she had at least closed the garage door and turned on the flood lights he installed to illuminate the property.

As Charlotte reached the truck, she paused. *Of course it is a single row of seats. You are killing me, Ruth.* She sighed and opened the door. She had gotten some pretty good practice climbing in and out of Todd's truck, and Luke's wasn't as high, so she made it up and in on her first try. *Success!* She scooted over into the middle, figuring the sooner they were at the game, the sooner she could get out.

Ruth climbed in beside her, effortlessly. *Apparently that is something that does get easier with practice*, Charlotte mused. As Luke slid in the driver side, he handed her the second tub of cookies. She bit her lip to keep from smiling as he fumbled with his seatbelt. Finally, the buckle clicked. What was only a couple of seconds had felt like hours of him fumbling near her left hip.

"Shall we?" Luke asked his passengers with a smile.

CHARLOTTE COULD PRACTICALLY FEEL her face getting sunburned. *Really smart, Charlie. Wasn't the hike enough to remind you how easily you burn?* When they drove past the bank, the display flashed eighty-five degrees. Charlotte finished her third bottle of water and watched what she hoped was the last inning. *How many innings is a softball game again? Seven? Maybe nine?* Charlotte spent the first part of the game shadowing Ruth and feeling completely out of place as the women managed the food and fussed over each others' "secret recipes." The women were very welcoming, and Charlotte started to see why small towns were so alluring to other people. She finally sat down to watch the game. Then, a shadow fell over her as a young woman walked up and sat beside her.

"Hi there, you must the Charlotte everyone is talking about. I'm Mandy." She smiled, and Charlotte turned to her. *Voice is slightly strained, eyes a little too wide... She's trying awfully hard to seem friendly. Pulse is elevated, jaw clenched behind the smile.* The read on Mandy was instinctual, and took less than the time it took to screw the top back on her water bottle. *She feels threatened.*

Charlotte gave her biggest smile. "Nice to meet you, Mandy. Are you cheering for anyone in particular?"

Mandy laughed, the sound high pitched and squeaky. Mandy tucked her curly brown hair behind one ear. "You are too precious. Of course you wouldn't know, but, I'm cheering for Luke."

"Oh?" Charlotte faltered. *Of course you are.* "That's great. His team is doing pretty well. At least, I think they are. I don't know much about softball," she said laughing. *Easiest way to put someone at ease is to let them underestimate you.*

Mandy nodded. "They are doing great. Looks like they almost have the game in the bag." They sat in silence for a few seconds while a batter from the

Catholic church swung at a pitch, whiffed, and took some encouragement from his buddies on the bench. He hit a line-drive on the next pitch and headed around the bases. "So, where are you staying?" Mandy asked.

Voice inflection is too heavy. She knows the answer to the question, but doesn't like it. Again, Charlotte's evaluation was habit. These were the types of conversations she was used to. A power struggle, where both parties thought they had the upper hand. She answered truthfully, "I moved into Miss Ruth's cabin last week."

Mandy nodded absently as she studied Luke at shortstop, "I've heard it is a nice place. I know Luke has worked very hard on it."

"You've never seen it?"

Mandy stopped breathing. And then exhaled. "I just haven't seen it all fixed up. Luke was waiting to show me until it was completely finished. I guess Miss Ruth decided it was ready enough for you."

Remembering the conversation she had over-heard between Luke and Ruth, she smiled. "That is exactly what happened." *Maybe I should just tell her that Luke was still spending a lot of time fixing it up, but now he had an audience.* Charlotte didn't think Mandy would appreciate that. Instead, Charlotte just continued, "It was almost done, and Luke hasn't been around much. He doesn't seem thrilled to have a tenant in his pet project." *If she wants Luke, or already has him, more power to her. I can't imagine wanting to see him more than I already do. It feels like he is around constantly.*

It didn't take her long to catch on to Luke's evening routine of closing up Ruth's house. The first night, when she heard a car door, she grabbed a skillet to use as a weapon, thinking no one in their right mind would be visiting Miss Ruth at that time of night. When she saw it was Luke's truck, she slinked back to her cottage.

Then, she remembered last night. She heard Luke make his normal rounds at the main house, but then she could have sworn he walked down to the cottage as well. Like any good city girl, she kept her doors locked all the time. *Probably just a dream,* she reminded herself. *Luke doesn't care if you get robbed. Why would he?*

Mandy's smile relaxed after hearing that Luke and Charlotte weren't becoming fast friends. Chrissy walked up and joined them, and the three of them watched the end of the game together. Baptists 8, Catholics 5. The teams high-fived and slapped each other on the shoulder after the game, and everyone met back near home plate, closest to the bleachers. Charlotte had been briefed on this between being peppered with questions from Ruth's friends during the first couple of innings. After the game, tradition dictated that the winning team prayed for the ministry and men of the losing team, and the meal. The pastor from the Baptist church spoke with a booming voice to get everyone's attention. Then, he asked Luke to say the prayer.

Luke nodded and caught her eye before closing his. "Father, thank you for this community. As many times as I thank you for these people, it is not enough for the blessing that they are. Thank you that we can come together and fellowship. Please, continue to bless our lives with deep relationships that find their connection in You. Father, I thank you for the men of this community, from every walk of life that are working every day to be the men you call us to be. I am so grateful that regardless of which church we sit in on Sunday mornings, we all worship You - the one and only God - every day." His warm voice rang out clearly over the crowd, and Charlotte listened to the words carefully. Her life had never included anyone who prayed out loud. Luke continued, "I ask that you continue to bless the ministry and outreach of the Catholic church here in Minden. That they would look to you for encouragement and direction and that you would give them a heart for reaching people for you. I ask the same for my church. That you would challenge us and continue to present us with opportunities to show your love to the world. Bless this food to our bodies and the loving hands that prepared it. Thank you, Father, for the wonderful support of this community. For these old friends and those becoming our new friends. It is in your precious Son's Holy name we come before you, Amen."

Charlotte's eyes flew open when he said the part about new friends. Sure enough, when he finished praying, he looked at her and winked. *He does not think we are becoming friends. And he did not just wink at me!* Unfortunately, she was pretty sure he had. And, even worse, she was pretty sure she'd blushed.

IT SEEMED as though the entire town was there. The line for dinner was long; even with the men insisting that all the women were served first. The losing team was relegated to serving duty; dishing out burgers, hotdogs, and pulled pork before handing the plates to each person. Charlotte found herself at the end of the line with Chrissy; Mandy having wandered off after the prayer. Charlotte asked for pulled pork and then filled her plate with pasta salad, deviled eggs, fruit, and cheesy potatoes. She made sure to grab one of Miss Ruth's cookies before sitting down beside Chrissy at one of the picnic tables.

Before long, Todd joined them. Hoping to give them some time alone, Charlotte got up to grab an extra napkin and something to drink. She stood debating between iced tea and lemonade when Luke came up beside her. "Go with the lemonade," he said absently. "Marsha Baker makes it from scratch every year. It's the best you'll ever have."

She studied him before answering. "If you insist. I don't think I've ever had fresh squeezed lemonade before." She grabbed the cup the first baseman from the Catholic team had filled for her. "Good game today, Luke."

"It was a lot of fun, everybody played hard."

"Especially you." She had watched him during the game. Shortstop was a demanding position, and he was involved in a lot of the plays. She had seen him coaching some of the other players after they made mistakes. He was competitive but had never gotten upset when he or a teammate had made a mistake. She saw him shake his head after striking out one at-bat; but then giving a good-natured smile to the batter up after him. She was used to men in the business world; cutthroat and often cross when things did not go as planned; if not overtly irate. His easy-going nature was refreshing. Of course, it was very different than what she had seen when she first met him and he was trying to have her evicted before she even moved in. Charlotte tried to remind herself of that guy. *Maybe it will help me remember he isn't perfect after all.*

"I try to give my all. Sometimes it works out, I guess." She knew he was being modest. He had helped two double plays and hit a triple with two guys on base.

"Well, today it did." Charlotte started to walk away from him. He followed.

"Mind if I sit with you?"

She stopped abruptly and looked at him. "Won't Mandy mind? She's over at that table trying to get your attention." Charlotte had seen the woman craning her neck to watch their conversation and get Luke's attention without being too obvious.

Luke's gut reaction – annoyance - was so fleeting, most probably would have missed it. Charlotte noted it and was surprised by her own reaction of relief.

What do you care if they are together? He responded quickly, "No, she won't mind." If Charlotte hadn't seen the split-second tightening of the jaw and downward twitch of his eyebrows, she would have never guessed it wasn't the truth.

"Okay... We're over here." She led him back to her table, where Chrissy and Todd were laughing. She noted absently the body language of the two. They were leaned toward each other across the table, and Chrissy had her hand on the table beside her plate in his direction. *Oh yeah, they are definitely into each other,* she thought with a smile.

Charlotte took a bite of Miss Ruth's cookie. "Wow. Your mom makes a mean cookie."

Luke looked at her strangely. "My mom? Oh, you mean Ruth? She's actually my mother-in-law."

Charlotte's mind whirled as she processed this new information. "But, you call her 'Mom' and neither of you ever mentioned that you are married!" Now she was furious. And embarrassed about the inappropriate thoughts she'd been having all afternoon watching Luke play baseball. Where on earth was his wife? Why wasn't she here?

"I'm sorry, Charlotte. I thought you knew. I married Ruth's daughter, Rachel, seven years ago, but she died in a car accident two years ago." He spoke the last phrase softly, so only she could hear. Luke looked away in what Charlotte interpreted as a move of self-preservation. The glimpse before he turned away from her showed pain and sorrow in his eyes.

Charlotte's stomach dropped. "Oh my. I'm so sorry. I had no idea. I just... assumed you were her son. You and Miss Ruth are so close."

His lips quirked up into an small involuntary smile. "Yeah, Ruth's the best. She's the closest thing to a real mom I've got."

After the softball game, Charlotte spent the evening at the cottage. She considered the revelation of Luke as Ruth's son-in-law. She replayed every one of their conversations and re-evaluated his reactions with the new context. He had been married. And not that long ago. Charlotte considered the effect of losing a wife when you were in your mid-20s. It wasn't surprising that he held himself at a distance. Clearly, there was something about this cottage that was a sore point for him. Maybe this is where Rachel lived? Or maybe where they had lived together?

No wonder he doesn't want me here. This was their place. Charlotte considered the kind gestures he made today. He didn't hate her anymore, at least she didn't think he did. Today, all of the sudden, Luke was polite and friendly. He had winked at her during the prayer for crying out loud! But what did that mean? His first few encounters sure indicated Luke wasn't over his wife. Maybe he had decided that he and Charlotte could be friends.

She could be friends, right? *Sure, I'll have no problem being just friends with the handsome, kind, funny, complicated son-in-law of my landlord. What could go wrong?*

In the evenings, she read books from Miss Ruth's extensive library. Occasionally she met up with Todd or Chrissy, or even their whole group of friends for dinner or drinks or games. Luke was around, but not often. She saw him at Ruth's, and occasionally he was out with the group. Mostly, she just heard him doing his nightly check of the house and the cottage, and she found herself never really falling asleep fully until she knew his evening ritual was complete.

In the mornings, she woke up later than she used to, waiting for the sun to wake her naturally. *No alarm clocks while I'm on sabbatical,* she had promised herself the very first week. And so far, the rude report of a clock radio or cell phone alarm had not interrupted her dreams at all. She sat with a mug of tea on the front porch of the cottage, listening to the woods come alive around her. She was free to spend her days doing whatever she wanted. No more baking, though. At least not without Ruth's help and supervision. Charlotte remembered all the things she used to do with the seemingly extinct creature of 'free-time'.

She visited Miss Ruth often, and the two of them gardened and baked and Charlotte attempted to crochet. But mostly they just talked, like they were doing today.

Ruth asked tons of questions and loved to hear about Charlotte's life. "What was your favorite place in the whole world to visit, so far?"

Charlotte considered her answer. "Well, I've always loved Europe. I usually end up in big cities, because that's where companies are located. I didn't hate Paris like some people do, and Munich is beautiful. Bern in Switzerland was one of my favorites, and I love the hustle and bustle of London. Probably, though..." She grew contemplative and admitted to Ruth, "My favorite place in the whole world was a little farm village on the northwest coast of France in Normandy. It's called Saint-Pierre-en-Port."

"Why there?" Unlike so many people Charlotte

had met, when Ruth asked questions, she really seemed to care about the answer. Ruth's eyes were deep pools of emotion, filled with love and compassion.

"I don't really know. Maybe when I was there, I really needed what it had to offer. Less than a thousand people live there. They farm and fish, and they welcomed me, even though I was clearly an outsider. I didn't do anything but walk the trails along the cliffs. They are the French side of the white cliffs of Dover", she explained. Charlotte smiled, continuing, "It was beautiful. No cell phone, no computer, and almost no one knew I was there. I guess in a way, it is a lot like here."

Ruth laughed, "Minden with a view, I suppose."

Charlotte grinned in agreement. "Well, with a view, and buildings that are hundreds of years old."

"I can't believe how many places you have been." Ruth shook her head.

"I suppose. I've been a lot of places, but I've only seen a few. Does that make sense?"

Charlotte realized it was true. When she traveled for work, schedules were always jam-packed. Flights backed up to interviews which backed up to long dinners and more flights. She'd never taken the time to add vacation days onto trips like some of her coworkers. Instead, she'd always gotten back to the office as soon as possible.

"Do you think you'll go back?" Somehow, Charlotte knew Ruth wasn't talking about Europe, but was referring to her old life and her career.

Charlotte's eyes fell. "I don't know. Part of me needs to go back. And part of me never wants to take those kind of risks again." She paused. *Should I tell her? Will she think badly of me if she knows the truth?* Charlotte studied Miss Ruth, and saw nothing but love and acceptance and curiosity in her eyes. "I was fired. Well, not really fired – but 'encouraged to pursue other opportunities.'" She put up finger quotes on the last part. "It was humiliating."

Gently, Ruth prodded. "Can I ask what happened?"

Charlotte sighed. "To really understand what happened, we have to go back to the beginning." Ruth gestured for her to continue. "I worked with Anna for ten years... I even considered us friends. We started at Millennium at the same time, both of us right out of college. Millennium is a consulting firm that specializes in corporate talent. Everything from teaching companies how to recruit from universities, to performing interviews and psych evaluations for companies hiring high-level executives. Turns out, I'm pretty good at reading people."

Charlotte gave a quiet, cynical laugh. "I became the highest grossing specialist in the executive talent office. A lot of those contracts have extended payoff clauses tied to the success of the candidate. I started being specifically requested based on reputation. It wasn't that Anna wasn't a good psychologist or that she wasn't good at her job… but I could see things she couldn't. Micro-expressions that revealed something a candidate was trying to hide. Once you know someone is hiding something, it's a matter of pushing the right buttons to get them to tell you." She shook her head, trying to explain to Ruth the power she'd held.

"I bet I know secrets about every executive on the Fortune 500 list… We were working on a hire for Byte; the tech company. They needed a new corporate development officer. The board of directors had actually given us a short list of candidates. Two internal, and three external. And they had specifically requested I take the lead. I asked Anna to assist, since it was a pretty big case; with a lot of potential for sensitive information about potential mergers and product developments. I trusted her."

Charlotte paused, and looked up at Ruth.

She hesitated, then blurted out, "Anna sabotaged the process. I think she lied about what was in the candidates' psych evaluations and what she had found during the research phase. She basically made me look incompetent. Turns out, she had been doing it for months. Everyone thought I had lost my edge. I guess maybe I had. I didn't see what she was doing. I never even suspected! It was my job to know when people were lying and I couldn't even tell my closest colleague was screwing me over!" She stopped, tried to hold in the tears threatening to spill over her eyelashes.

Ruth was shaking her head. "Oh honey, it's not your fault. Trusting the wrong person doesn't make you a failure. It just makes you human." She waited for Charlotte to look up again. "Why did you leave?"

"The last straw was a very sensitive document from our client being leaked to the press. I was the only one with access to it. But I swear, I would never have done that. My boss made me take a leave of absence. The stress of the situation started giving me anxiety attacks. I couldn't even try to prove what Anna had done. My therapist said I should take a break. Spend some time somewhere else before I try to make a comeback. And that's how I ended up in Minden. That's how I ended up with you." Charlotte realized she hadn't thought about going back in several days. *I have to go back, who am I without my job?*

"I'm pretty sure God brought you here, Charlotte. I know you don't believe that yet. But I feel it." Ruth spoke with such conviction, Charlotte was almost convinced. If God brought her here, it meant God cared. And if God really cared, why would he have let Anna destroy her career? It was a circle she couldn't reason her way out of.

9

Charlotte continued to keep her distance from Luke, despite seeming to run into him everywhere. When she went to Ruth's, he would stop by. If she went to the QuikStop for a lemonade, he would be putting gas into his muddy green pickup. And if she laid in bed with the lights off and listened to the cicadas and the crickets, there he was. Plodding down from the main house, to check the locks on her little cottage before finding his way back up the narrow wooden staircase to the main driveway and Ruth's house. Charlotte listened until she heard him turn on his truck and drive away. There was something about this evening ritual that made her inexplicably happy. She didn't know Luke, not really. She knew Ruth, and she knew some of

Luke's friends. And she even knew that he had married Ruth's daughter, Rachel, and that she had died two years ago. She knew he worked as a landscaper and that he was kind and thoughtful and boyishly charming, when he wasn't being stubborn and sarcastic. Knowing that this man, even though Charlotte had invaded the cabin where his memories lived was checking on her every night had her resisting the urge to melt into her pillow with a dreamy smile every night. Therefore, whenever Charlotte saw him out in town, or weeding the gardens at Ruth's – she was about as warm and cuddly as she'd ever been with the waiter at her favorite restaurant. *I acknowledge your existence. I am even kind of grateful you are here. But we are not friends.* She nodded at him, and if pushed (usually by Ruth) she would say hello and exchange the obligatory "how are you" small talk.

On Saturdays; Todd, Chrissy, Mandy, and some other friends went out to the only restaurant in town other than the diner—the Bulldog Bar and Grill. Charlotte had a standing invitation to join as well. She decided to join them after having been in Minden for a few weeks. When Charlotte asked about the name of the establishment, she was informed that back when Minden had its own high school, they were the Minden Bulldogs. The three closest high schools had consolidated about fifteen years back. The name of the bar was the only thing that remained.

As she listened to Mark telling a funny story about one of the middle schoolers he taught, Charlotte looked around the room. She felt more than saw Luke walk in and approach their table. Greetings from the others filled the air as he walked around the table pulled up a seat across from her. His gaze met hers and he looked at her expectantly.

She raised an eyebrow, "What?"

He chuckled. "Hello, Charlotte, it's good to see you too."

She rolled her eyes and blushed, properly admonished. "Hey, Luke."

The conversation on the other end of the table picked back up with others chiming in about their embarrassing middle school crushes and mishaps. Luke took the opportunity of semi-private conversation to ask Charlotte some of the questions he'd been saving. Her indifference to him was getting under his skin. When he asked Ruth questions about her, she simply shook her head and told him he'd better ask those questions himself. With her stuck at the table across from him for the evening, he saw his chance and took it.

"What did you do before you came to Minden?" He was curious about that. She'd finally ditched the creases in her jeans, but it was still silky tops and heels strapped to her ankles. She didn't exactly fit in Minden, but then again – her presence also no longer set him off like nails on a chalkboard. She stood out here, just slightly more polished. Slightly more well-spoken. Her being here wasn't like an askew puzzle piece like it had been originally, but Luke wasn't sure if it was her edges that had been softened or if the whole of Minden had shifted around to make room for the new piece.

Charlotte looked back at him but remained silent. He waited for her to answer. Instead, she gestured to the table beside them. "What do you see at that table?"

Luke leaned in and glanced over, willing to play along. "I guess I see a mother and father, and two happy kids."

Charlotte nodded, "What else?" She saw much more than the simple explanation he offered, and as always, was hoping that someone else could see it too. But they never did. Not at first.

"What do you mean? What else is there to see?"

"For one, the father is about 30 seconds from losing his temper with the kid who is on his Gameboy. He's been looking at him and gritting his teeth. He keeps looking at his wife, but isn't getting any backup. Two, the wife clearly has a favorite son – the one with the blue shirt. Her smile is more genuine every time she looks at him. The bags under her eyes are disguised with makeup. She's exhausted – maybe didn't sleep last night, but hiding it from everyone. The son – the favorite one – he is trying to be good, but he is coveting his dad's French fries while he eats the fruit ordered as his side. Mom and Dad haven't said two words to each other in ten minutes."

Right on cue, the father suddenly grabbed the Gameboy from his son's hands and leaned in to lecture him in a quiet, stern voice.

Charlotte looked back at Luke. "I read people, Luke. I notice things. Or, at least I used to."

Luke looked confused. "Do it again."

She complied, pointing out an adorably awkward high school couple on what appeared to be a first date, and then dissecting the dynamics within the group of young 20-something females cheering over a toast – who was the 'alpha', and who felt like she didn't belong.

"In a group of women like that, there is always a

ringleader. Someone whose presence at the event essentially dictates its collective success or failure. Sometimes it is extremely obvious and plans never solidify until that friend confirms their availability. Sometimes, most of the group isn't even aware that it works like this. The leader? They've never known it any other way. It is normal to them to be the center of attention. See the girl with the blonde hair in a ponytail?" Luke acknowledged the one she was talking about. "She is friends with the brunette next to her, and the blonde across the table – the one with the red shirt. But she either hadn't met any of the other women before tonight or isn't close with them at all. See how she never interjects into the conversation? Except when - yep, just like that – she says something directly to one of her friends, never to the group as a whole."

"How do you see all that? She looks like she is having fun with the group."

"She is having fun, but she isn't part of the group. At least not yet." Then, Charlotte studied a couple at a table across the crowded room. They sat close, his hand on her arm. At first glance, they looked like a couple on a date, enjoying their time together. But Charlotte noticed things others wouldn't. The man's eyes were a little too wide, and the woman's smile was frozen in place. She was trying to hide it but she was terrified. Charlotte's gaze shifted to his hand on her arm and saw it tighten a little more. Looking at Luke, she found him watching her. "Luke, we have to do something."

He frowned. "What do you mean?"

"That table over there. Something's not right. She doesn't want to be here with him."

Luke looked over his shoulder and located the table she mentioned. "Everything looks okay to me, are you sure?"

Charlotte started to get agitated. Her abilities were sometimes a curse. "Please, you have to do something. She's scared. Look at her eyes, Luke." She pleaded with the man across from her. "Just her eyes. And look how tight he is holding her arm."

Luke's jaw clenched and his eyes fluttered closed. When they opened, he was already standing up. "Come on, then."

They walked to the table and immediately, Charlotte saw the grateful look in the woman's eyes. Responding to the emotion etched on the woman's face, Charlotte jumped in.

"Oh, wow! I never would have expected to see you here!" Charlotte gave the stranger a reassuring smile and then looked at the man across the table. He didn't look happy to be interrupted. "Oh, where are my manners? I'm Charlotte, her cousin."

The woman grabbed her arm and pulled her down to the table, "I'm so glad you are here, Charlotte!"

"We really should catch up. You don't mind, do you Ray?" Without giving him a chance to protest, Charlotte kept talking, spinning a story that would get them out of the situation. "I have to get home to the kids, but why don't you come over and have a cup of coffee?"

Ray started to protest, but Luke dismissed him with an overly firm handshake. "Nice to meet you Ray. I'm sure your date will be in touch."

Charlotte and Luke ushered her outside and the woman introduced herself as Jessica.

"Thank you so much. I don't know what I would have done." Jessica shivered. "He seemed harmless enough when we chatted online. I'm such an idiot."

"You are not," Charlotte protested. "You were smart to meet him someplace busy like Bulldogs. Just be careful, okay? There's a lot of creeps out there."

Luke was silent through the exchange.

What are you thinking, Luke? Do you wish you hadn't asked the question? Maybe seeing the world like I do makes faith impossible.

After Jessica was safely in her car and on her way, they lingered outside. The night was warm and quiet. Luke stood, with his eyes dark and his hands in his pockets. Charlotte knew they were fisted tightly, as she watched his forearm muscles tense. "Luke?" Her quiet question interrupted the calm. When he didn't respond, she added, "I'm sorry."

His head lifted quickly. "You're sorry? What are you sorry for?" He sounded genuinely perplexed. "You may have saved that woman. Only God knows what might have happened if it had escalated further. You were amazing. Charlotte, look at me." She looked. He started walking toward her. "God sent you here, to Jessica, tonight. I'm grateful I was there, but sweetheart – he sent **you.**" He emphasized the last word and as he reached her, he took her hand.

"Thank you, Father, for protecting Jessica tonight. For Charlotte's willingness to help where she saw a need. You are so good, Amen."

Charlotte was speechless. *He called me sweetheart. He called me **sweetheart**? And then he prayed... While holding my hand?* Immediately, her thoughts went back to St. Louis. She flipped through all the reasons she couldn't get involved with Luke, not the least of which was that she wasn't staying.

Not forever. And Luke was definitely a forever kind of guy.

Uncomfortable, she pulled her hand from his as the restaurant door opened and the family she had analyzed trickled out. She sighed. "I was a psychologist, Luke. An exceptionally observant one. Like earlier – I said I was sorry because you were upset. I could see the muscles in your jaw clench, and your forearms tighten. Your eyes were narrowed. And you were upset. But then, I said I was sorry and you weren't upset with me. So why? I don't understand." *I need to understand. Am I really that that far off my game? He WAS upset. What other reason could there have been except he didn't want to be pulled into this?*

Luke clicked his tongue. "I've always been told I was hard to read... but you are right. I was upset. But I wasn't angry with you. I was angry with the situation. With myself for not seeing what you saw so clearly. With the man who couldn't accept that a woman wanted nothing to do with him. I wanted to walk back into Bulldogs and find Jessica's date and teach him a lesson." He smiled wryly. "I was about to... until you said my name. Then it evaporated."

After a beat, Charlotte said what she had been thinking for minutes. "You called me sweetheart'..."

she tried to sound accusing, but she only sounded curious. Having his attitude toward her shift so dramatically over the last few weeks had really confused her.

He looked struck. "I did?" After the shock, Charlotte saw pain in his eyes.

"Yeah." Her lame reply hung in the air between them.

Luke looked away, eyes down and to the left. After a beat, he said, "I should really go. Do you have a ride?"

Charlotte blinked at the subject change. "Umm, yeah. I'm good." Luke was absolutely crazy. One minute he tells her to leave town and never come back, and the next he calls her sweetheart and holds her hand. And then he's back to stilted sentences and chilly words. Charlotte was exhausted even trying to keep track of where she stood with him.

"Okay, then. Goodnight, Charlotte."

Charlotte stood alone in the light of the single streetlamp and watched him walk away.

10

_____

Chrissy and Charlotte struck up a friendship after that day in the diner when Luke had been so cruel, and Charlotte often met her at the café while Chrissy took a break when it was slow. Chrissy sipped her coffee and joked about her parent's refusal to put up a Facebook page for the cafe.

"I'm so tempted to just do it without them knowing."

"Why don't you? Chrissy, you'd be a great marketing manager!"

"That's okay. I'm fine just being a waitress." Charlotte heard the tinge of a lie that Chrissy wanted to believe. Chrissy was easy to like, with her big smile and cheerful demeanor. Every now and then, Charlotte caught the underlying self-doubt or melancholy that she knew was normal for everyone. She wasn't sure of the root of it in Chrissy's case.

Not yet, anyway. Charlotte always asked if Todd had made a move yet, with Chrissy's inevitable response being "ugh, no. I don't understand that man."

It seemed that Todd was the only person in the entire town that couldn't see how Chrissy felt about him, or if he did know, he refused to act on it. If she'd been the meddling type, Charlotte would have confronted him and told him to get his act together. He'd readily admitted his feelings about Chrissy to Charlotte shortly after they met. She wasn't sure why he was dragging his feet. Charlotte's intuition told her there was much more to Todd than met the eye. He acted carefree and told self-deprecating jokes. But the lovable jock had undercurrents of thoughtfulness and intelligence he wasn't showing the world. Charlotte hadn't figured out why. The temptation to analyze her friends was always there and her defenses were always up, looking for dishonesty.

Charlotte tried to avoid talking about Luke as much as possible, but Chrissy always brought him up. He and Charlotte were still being cordial, even likely able to be classified as friendly acquaintances.

Charlotte never had many friends, so she was hesitant to call Luke one. At least they no longer scowled at each other, so that was progress.

Chrissy loved to hear about Charlotte's past life. She herself had never been far outside of Minden, but she loved reading about other places.

"I think the world is a fascinating place, I just love Minden too much to leave!"

The nugget of information niggled at Charlotte and she pushed harder. "Even for a short trip? You could come right back after a week exploring someplace else?"

"Why would I need to leave, when I can watch videos and read books? It's way cheaper and I can see so much from right here?" Chrissy explained her reasoning as though she had done so a hundred times before. "Plus, I don't have to deal with the hassle of airports or train stations."

This mentality didn't make any sense to Charlotte, who had never once considered reading a book about Ireland an acceptable substitute to actually seeing it. Charlotte caught indications of falsehoods in some of Chrissy's thoughts about travel but was careful not to push her new friend too far. It was a mistake she had made too many times in the past, costing her friendships far before they were deep enough to survive the onslaught of her interrogation. She could see that Chrissy was adamant about not leaving Minden was very much true, regardless of the true reason behind the position.

One morning, as Chrissy and Charlotte were enjoying their coffee, Mandy waltzed into the café and over to their table. Charlotte hadn't seen her since the softball game. She knew Chrissy was friends with her though, so she attempted to slide her chair across the weathered linoleum to make room for Mandy to join them.

Mandy was cordial to Charlotte, if not overly friendly. Charlotte learned that Mandy ran an in-home daycare in Minden and spent her days corralling toddlers. She took one day a month off and her mom filled in for her at the daycare so she could have a break to go to a doctor or hair appointment. Upon hearing this, Charlotte exclaimed honestly, "I don't know how you do that! I can't imagine being surrounded by kids all day, and not even your own kids at that." Charlotte quickly saw the flash of sadness in Mandy's eyes at the mention of her lack of own children. Kicking herself, she added, "what do you do all day with them?"

Mandy talked through the daily schedule, explaining that she taught preschool lessons to the kids, so they learned letters, numbers, days and months, but also concepts like outer space or the oceans.

Charlotte was impressed. After their initial meeting, she had painted Mandy as a shallow man-trap, but this was a whole other side. Charlotte quickly revised her mental file folder about Mandy and noted the organization skills and the profession-alism and pride that Mandy took in her work at the daycare. Was it so hard to understand that Mandy had been threatened by Charlotte's arrival? It didn't seem like Luke was interested, but Mandy seemed to have had high hopes where he was concerned. However, Mandy's demeanor here today, even after Charlotte and Luke had talked most of the night at the bar while she was only a few feet away, was friendly and Charlotte was glad to see she wasn't holding a grudge. Maybe Mandy could be another friend.

One thing her conversations with Chrissy, Mandy, and Ruth revealed was their steadfast faith and sense of purpose. Each of them had seen hard-ships and setbacks in life. But they spoke of God's blessings regularly and without sarcasm. Charlotte sometimes felt like her additions to the conversations only served to further set her apart. She avoided any questions that were intrusive or rude, but the truth she saw on their faces spoke for itself. Ruth was truly at peace with losing her daughter and her husband. She believed wholeheartedly that God was active and interested in her life.

For Charlotte, the idea seemed nuttier than a bag of cashews. But she couldn't help but wish she had that kind of foundation. Instead, her foundation was a couple of drug-addicted losers and sisters she'd never see again. Mandy admitted her loneliness, confirming the sadness Charlotte had detected when she asked Mandy about children of her own. But despite Mandy's unfulfilled desire for a husband and children, she seemed to know that God was in control.

It seemed too easy to Charlotte. If God was in control, then what was the point of striving for anything? Or did the world just float along based on the whims of some benevolent dictator? As much as she loved being here in Minden and not having any of the pressures of her old life, she also felt aimless. Charlotte was coming to realize she'd always felt that way, and it was buried beneath piles of paperwork. It was easy to ignore the whisperings of insecurity when enjoying expensive client dinners and hopping red-eye flights to the West Coast. But here, endless hours of solitude stretched before her. And when Charlotte had that much time to think, it was impossible to ignore the things that she'd been running from.

At seventeen, Charlotte had fled her disaster of a family, afraid their failures meant she was destined to ruin things, too. More than ten years since then had been spent chasing a vision of success—as though she could prove herself better than her roots if she achieved enough in life. When that success had fallen apart, she'd run away from the ashes of her career. The betrayal of her best friend rocked her to her core and Charlotte was still convinced she should have seen it coming.

Without her career, Charlotte knew she didn't have anything. She didn't have the contentment Ruth wore like a handmade shawl. She didn't have the confidence Mandy rested in. Even Luke, having lost so much, had a family and a community in Minden. Charlotte only had her job as an executive recruiter. And even if she got it back, Charlotte was beginning to wonder if it would be enough.

11

Luke spent the next days avoiding Charlotte as best as he could. He successfully made his nighttime rounds at Ruth's late enough that Charlotte's lights were always off. He spent his days doing the backbreaking work of the landscaping business that he usually loved. Seeing the physical transformation that he made happen usually gave him a sense of accomplishment. He usually relished the time to think that the work allowed. But this week, it was driving him crazy. The late nights and early mornings surrounding warm days of building retaining walls were wearing him out. Since Charlotte had arrived, he'd struggled with conflicting emotions. He wanted her gone, because a part of him still died every time he saw her at the cabin. He wanted to be her friend, and to make her smile again. Charlotte didn't smile enough. Luke didn't want to like her, didn't want her to be friends with Todd and to be adopted by Ruth. Ruth was his. But actually, Ruth had adopted him just the same and he couldn't deny that acceptance and love to someone else who needed it. And the scariest feeling of all? He wanted to kiss her.

Why did you bring her here? I miss Rachel so much and yet I can't stop thinking about Charlotte. I called her sweetheart, Father. What does that mean? I'm so tired. I don't want to stay away, but I can't get close. What am I supposed to do?

Come to me, all who are weary and heavy laden; and I will give you rest.

I'm here, Abba. I'm here. Please show me what to do.

Pray without ceasing.

Pray for what?

But Luke didn't get an answer to that.

He prayed anyway. And he avoided the cottage. Except for five minutes every night when Luke checked her doors and prayed another wordless prayer. He never saw her during his rounds, but one night Charlotte caught him by surprise. Luke froze at the base of the steps when she spoke. "I haven't seen you much." She was closer than he expected – sitting on the porch with a cup of tea. Charlotte sounded tired and he ached to see her more clearly. Her green eyes and smooth skin haunted his dreams, but dreams were a poor substitute.

"I know. I've been busy." He sounded tired, too. *Lame excuse, man. She deserves the truth.* "Okay, that's not entirely true. I've been keeping myself busy so I wouldn't see you." Luke hung his head at the admission. What could he say? He had feelings for Charlotte. And Rachel had only been gone for two years.

She nodded. "I figured as much."

"I just..." He trailed off, then started again. "What do you know about my past?" He wondered how much Ruth had told her. Maybe she already knew everything and he wouldn't have to retell the painful story again.

"Nothing really. I know you were married to Ruth's daughter and that she died. But that's all."

Luke swallowed, debating what to tell her. Rachel was a part of him. More than that, Luke wasn't always sure who he was without her. "I was lost when I met Rachel. Kicked out of my parents' house when I was seventeen, I landed in Bloom-ington and was working as a grunt on the landscaping crew for the University. Rachel was a student." He sat on the step and looked up at the sky. "Thirty-thousand students on that campus and I only saw Rachel." Luke smiled at the memory. "Probably because she saw me. They all walked around and ignored us as we mulched and weeded and mowed. But not Rachel." He shook his head. "She said hello and smiled. Rachel asked about the flowers I was planting – I didn't even know the answers at that point. Eventually, we became friends. She was so happy, so full of life. I was addicted to being around her. She brought me to church." A choked laugh escaped from his throat. "I'd never stepped foot in a church before, but I would have followed her anywhere. When Thanksgiving rolled around, she found out I didn't have anywhere to go and she brought me home to Miss Ruth." He exhaled a laugh, then paused before continuing. "They saved my life. Miss Ruth and Rachel taught me about my Creator and my purpose. They loved me even though I was a screw up. A little while later, I became a Christian and I asked Rachel to marry me." He paused, and turned to look at Charlotte before admitting what had him tied up in knots all week. "I called her sweetheart, Charlotte. Only her."

Charlotte remained perfectly still.

Luke continued his story. Might as well get it all out. "We got married when she graduated, I was only 21. She and I lived in this cabin back then, back when we had nothing but each other. Five years later, she was killed in a car accident." He stopped there, unable to share the most painful part of the story. With every breath, Luke still mourned the baby his wife had been carrying the day she died.

Charlotte murmured, "Oh, Luke."

A tear rolled down his cheek, "I hated God for that. For taking her away. For a long time, I didn't realize that I had tied my salvation and worth so closely to hers. Without her, I was still lost. It's a long time for Miss Ruth to help me see that God wasn't to blame. I'm still working on it some days." He took a deep breath and composed himself. "I don't know why I'm telling you this, except to say – I think you might be lost too. And God knows I want to help. But I'm not sure I have what it takes. I'm not sure I can help you find answers without becoming so tangled up in you that I can't walk away. And I couldn't take it if you were the one to leave."

She set down her tea and moved to sit beside him on the stairs.

"I think I am lost, Luke." She put her hand on his

arm. "I've got so many questions I can't answer. But I'm not leaving."

He stopped breathing when she touched him. Luke looked at her closely, trying to see beyond the surface—to see what Charlotte would see if she looked. Her eyes studied him unreservedly. Luke's gaze dropped to her lips, slightly parted. Slowly, he touched his hand to her cheek and as though reflex, her eyes drifted closed. Without thinking, he leaned in and pulled her lips to his. She relaxed into him and he deepened the kiss. His tongue caressed her lips and she opened for him. Warm and sweet, she tasted like the honey from her tea. His world spun unpredicably, like a top about to topple, and he reluctantly pulled away and met her eyes. The desire he saw there made his abdomen tighten. "Go inside, Charlotte." Her expression changed to one of confusion. In response, he kissed her lightly again. "Please? I will call you tomorrow."

She nodded and stood. He smiled when he heard the door lock behind her. After she went inside, he sat on the porch steps for a long time, praying. *I'm sorry, Father – forgive me for not seeing the biggest need. She needs you, Lord. Help me show her you.*

Luke hung his head in his hands. *I don't know what to do with these feelings, Lord. I never thought another woman would touch my heart after Rachel. And she doesn't know you! What am I going to do? I know you say to not be unequally yoked. Am I praying for Charlotte's salvation selfishly? Do my motives matter if the end result is what you would have anyway?*

The blackness of the night didn't answer him. But that kiss had changed things. Luke could no longer ignore his feelings for Charlotte. His world had been dark and dull for too long, and the fiery outsider had brought back a light he thought gone forever. But what good was that light if he couldn't pursue it?

CHARLOTTE REPLAYED her conversation with Luke in her mind all night and all day. She had been tired of lying in bed listening to him do his nightly rounds. Knowing he was so close and yet a million miles away. She'd ambushed him on the porch and their conversation had been deeper than any other they'd had so far. She had so many questions about the things he said and about the kiss. *What did he mean he was lost? He said Ruth taught him about his purpose... What is my purpose?* She used to think it was to be the best industrial psychologist in the world. That seemed incredibly shallow to her now. But still, the urge to return to her previous life ate at her. At least there, she had purpose. Charlotte loved her days filled with books and yoga and not a single national newspaper. But she felt aimless. *I have no idea what to be without that piece of me. And I did love it – until it all fell apart. I miss the challenge of assignments and the satisfaction of a delivered report. Of seeing the impact my decisions have on something so much bigger than me. Isn't that my purpose? At least Luke has his landscaping business. Running your own business, I bet that is fulfilling.*

She had Luke's number from Ruth, so she texted him from the prepaid cell phone she had picked up in Terre Haute.

CW: It's Charlotte. Can I ask you a question?

LB: Anything.

CW: You said they helped you find your purpose. What is it?

Luke took a long time replying.

LB: My purpose is to glorify God with my actions and point people to Jesus.

Charlotte didn't know how to respond. She knew Luke was a Christian, she had heard him pray multiple times. But, she had never met anyone who expressed their entire reason for existing as being their faith. Charlotte thought it was just something people did. Go to church. Pray for someone sick. Give money to the poor. *What else is there? I believe in God, I guess. I mean, I've never spent much time thinking about it. But we had to get here somehow. That's always been good enough. Why does it feel like that's not enough anymore?*

Luke sat in the chair and tried to pay attention to the sermon. Ever since he had texted with Charlotte, he had been kicking himself for coming on too strong. She had opened the door for a conversation about God, and he had kicked the dang thing in on her. She hadn't answered his call later that night. Disappointed, Luke left a message, lamely inviting her to join him this morning at church. *Clearly, she didn't want to join you. Probably because you just hit her in the face with the revelation it took you years to figure out.* He tuned back into the sermon and said a quick prayer for focus and an open-heart.

As Pastor Justin talked about Paul and his deep abiding joy; Luke soaked it in. He remembered what he knew about Paul – the 'thorn in his side', the times he was imprisoned and he marveled again at the passage being shared. "In all things I have learned to be content." *Thank you, Father, for your peace and joy that passes all understanding. My Joy is in you, no matter what. You are all I need.*

It had been two years since Rachel died, and Luke was stilling coming to terms with God again. Without Rachel as an anchor, he was lost. He quickly fell out of the habit of daily prayer and reading and he all but ignored the well-meaning friends who reached out to offer comfort. What did they know about grief? The only person he didn't shut out entirely was Ruth. She was grieving too, of course, but she was so steadfast and serene. At times, Luke wanted to shake her and yell, "Don't you realize that she is GONE? And she is never coming back?!" but he knew it wouldn't do any good. Ruth was unshakeable. Slowly, he came to realize that the only reason Ruth seemed so content was because she still had Jesus. And Luke realized that he didn't; not really. Sure, he'd believed when Rachel was alive – but it wasn't Jesus that had saved him then. It was Rachel. She'd saved him, or so he'd always thought. Jesus was just an afterthought to his devotion to her. And when she was gone, the only thing that remained was a poor excuse for a relationship with God.

Luke was still struggling with Charlotte's presence. On one hand, he couldn't help but feel like he was betraying Rachel with his interest in the out-of-town visitor. His memories of Rachel in the cabin were becoming blurred with the images of Charlotte laughing hysterically as cake batter burned in the oven behind her, or of Charlotte stomping off into the woods in skimpy shorts after telling him off. The memories of Rachel - singing worship songs while washing dishes, stealing his hammer and nails to hang pictures when he hadn't gotten around to it soon enough - were so sweet. Sure, there were fights too. Rachel would get frustrated at him for leaving his socks in the living room. Once, he yelled at her for buying a new designer purse for $500 when he was barely breaking even in Brand New Landscaping. They were like any newlywed couple, praying for a family someday. Luke pushed that thought away firmly. Ruth told him that Charlotte needed a friend. And that was what he was going to be. That kiss outside the cottage? Definitely a one-time thing. It had to be.

12

———

Charlotte snuck into the church during the second worship song. Finding an empty seat near the back, she listened to the music and read the lyrics being projected onto the screen in front. Now, she focused on the words of the preacher. As he shared, she found herself listening eagerly.

"When we think of broken people, we think of addicts or the homeless. We think of circumstances that are horrible. But we don't often think of CEO's or celebrities. We forget that behind the fame and success and money, what this book," he lifted his Bible, "says about human nature is true. That brokenness is a symptom of the human nature. And the rich and famous among us are just as broken as the heroin addicts. Although Paul was facing awful circumstances – he was imprisoned, likely sick or injured. But Paul wasn't broken. In fact, he said 'In all things, I have learned to be content.' He said, 'when I am weak, then I am strong' because he found his strength and identity in Christ. That is a peace that is beyond understanding and beyond the things of this fallen world."

Charlotte slipped out during the prayer after the sermon and walked a few blocks to the park. It was completely empty. She mentally flipped through the rich and powerful people she had interviewed over the years. She never spent much time considering the presence of faith in the candidates she evaluated, but now all sorts of memories of conversations flashed through her mind. One in particular was a candidate she had interviewed for a Chief Operations Officer. Charlotte had ended up not recommending Joe for the position, having decided he wasn't competitive enough. When the decision was communicated to him, he reached out to her directly. That wasn't too unusual, people often wanted feedback and to express their disappointment. Charlotte had good relationships with the people she interviewed. It usually didn't last beyond the rejection from their employer. Sometimes they wanted to yell at her and justify why they should have been recommended. But this man had just thanked her for her time and let her know that he appreciated the feedback she had given, and the conversations they had. All in all, the encounter had confused Charlotte, and had confirmed what she had thought. He was completely at peace with not getting the position. Charlotte had even wondered if he had truly wanted it. Looking back though, she realized something new. It wasn't that Joe wasn't competitive or that he didn't want the job. It was the faith he had mentioned once or twice that led to a sense of peace and contentment regardless of the outcome of the process. On a whim, she looked up his number and called.

"This is Joe."

"Hi Joe, this is Charlotte Walters. I interviewed you about a year ago for the COO position at LenTech?"

"Ah, yes, of course. Nice to hear from you Charlotte. How are you?" She could hear the curiosity in his voice.

"Well, I've been better," she admitted. "I've taken a leave of absence from Millennium."

"Oh? What can I do for you then?" He sounded confused, but also concerned.

She bit her lip, debating how to broach the subject. "I just wanted to ask you... Why weren't you more upset about not getting the job?" Instead of ending there, Charlotte kept talking. "I mean, you should have been upset. It was everything you had been working for. You were the candidate the job was slated for, and then you didn't get it."

Joe took a second to reply. "I did want that position, Charlotte. I would have done an amazing job. But, I learned a long time ago that God's plans and our plans are often very different. And I also learned that His plans are infinitely better. After my initial disappointment of not getting the job, I realized that it meant He had something even bigger and better for me. And the fact is, he could take everything away- – and though it might be tougher to swallow, I know it would be the best thing for me."

Charlotte shook her head in refusal of the idea. "But how could taking everything away be better? Why would God take everything away if you weren't doing anything wrong?"

"I don't know, Charlotte. Could be His way of proving to me that I can rely on Him, and not to rely on myself. Did you know that because I didn't get the COO job, I retired early? My wife and I started a charity, which could never have happened while I was still working, and it is exactly what I am meant to be doing. I don't know what's happening in your world, Charlotte – but I know God has wonderful plans for you. I'll be praying you trust that is true."

Charlotte didn't know how to respond to that. She'd grown used to Ruth mentioning God openly and was even beginning to be more comfortable with prayer as a concept, but this was unexpected. "Thanks, Joe. Say hi to Noelle for me, and send me the name of your charity. I'd love to give to what I know is a worthy cause."

"I'll do that. Best of luck, Charlotte."

His words rattled around in her mind. *He could take everything away and it would be okay. Not just 'okay' but 'the best thing'.* She headed back to the church to pick up her Jeep. Luke was sitting on it; staring at the doors of the church. When he saw her out of the corner of his eye, he didn't move.

"You came?" He was still staring at the church.

"I came," she confirmed.

Finally, he looked at her. Her breath caught at the intensity in his eyes. "I hoped you would." He said it so softly, she almost didn't hear him.

Choosing to ignore the growing desire to go to him, she instead responded lamely, "Thanks for inviting me. I better get going."

Luke nodded and stood. He watched her get in the truck and drive away. *She came. Praise the Lord! God, did you see that? She came!* Luke wasn't exactly sure when it had become so important to him that Charlotte go to church and become a Christian. It just was. Before anything else could happen with them, he needed to know she shared his faith. It was everything to him, his only anchor in a crazy world that had knocked him down too many times before he even turned twenty. Yet, Luke felt an unbelievable connection to her. Even when he practically wanted to throw her out of his precious cabin, where his memories of Rachel lived. He had immediately wanted to tousle her perfectly coiffed hair and splash some mud on those ironed jeans. Could Charlotte find happiness here, with him? Luke thought she could, but it wasn't about his presence. It was that he thought, just maybe, she could find God here too. That she'd realize how loved she was and that her gift of reading people was exactly that – a gift! Luke wanted that for her. More than he realized until he had noticed her leaving church, terrified Charlotte was leaving without a word because she thought it was hokey, or because it made her angry. As soon as he saw her walking back, he knew that wasn't the case, though. Luke might not be an expert at reading micro-expressions or body-language, but Charlotte looked deep in thought and slightly confused. Remembering his own struggle with faith, he figured that was progress more than anything.

13

Charlotte spent the afternoon sitting on her porch, simultaneously enjoying the quiet and wishing she had a distraction from her current thoughts. Her mind was a merry-go-round of topics. She thought about Luke and her conversation with Joe. Thinking about Joe made her think about Millennium and Anna and the fiasco with Byte. Which made her think about why she was in Minden and how she had met Ruth. Thinking about Ruth made her think about God, and of course, that led her back to Luke again.

In her time in Minden, she'd successfully avoided dwelling on the situation back in St. Louis as best as she could. The anger and self-doubt stayed away until she laid in bed and tried to fall asleep. It was in these moments she re-lived the conversation of Roger had with her after the development plan was leaked.

"Charlie, you haven't been yourself for months now. Your success rate is way down, companies are calling and asking for money back on their fees. I've been patient. I figured it was a phase. I figured someone broke your heart or you had something going on at home. And now this?" He turned his laptop around to the front page of TechNews where the headline splashed, "Byte's top-secret develop plan leaked: investments in Bitcoin and self-driving cars". I can't believe you would do this to me, after all we've been through. At the worst – you intentionally leaked one of the most critical documents one of our customers have ever entrusted to us. At best, you are so far from the detailed, organized psychologist I mentored that you carelessly handled this document and ruined your future in the process."

By this time in the conversation, Charlotte had been biting her lip hard enough to draw blood to keep from crying. "I didn't, Roger, I didn't do anything. You have to understand."

"Look Charlotte, I tried. I gave you the benefit of the doubt for over a year now. But this? I can't let this go. My company is on the line. MINE. I need you to leave. I won't fire you, because call-me-crazy, I still want you to come back and be the best executive recruiter I've ever seen. But you have to leave and deal with whatever it is that has you so turned around. You've hardly taken a vacation in the eight years you've been here, so I'm ordering you to do so. An official leave of absence."

The worst part of it was knowing that she wasn't turned around. She was as good as she'd ever been, that was true – but something had been off. The candidates never seemed as good as she wanted them to any more, and while she always selected the best one – she wasn't usually surprised when they didn't work out. Her only clue came when she was packing up her office. Her friend, Anna, had stopped in to say good-bye. But what Charlotte realized was that there was no sympathy, no concern in her eyes or voice. There was only well-disguised happiness and a pulse – visible to discerning eyes on Anna's slender neck – that was elevated with excitement. In that moment, Charlotte knew that she had been duped. And though her leave of absence felt more permanent every day she stayed in Minden, she had to take back her reputation. Which is about how far she got during every repeat of this thought parade before asking herself the question she just didn't know how to answer. *How did she do it? And how can I prove it to Roger?*

Today, though, she thought about God and Luke. How everything the pastor had said made sense to her. How the CEOs and celebrities she'd met were really just people. She'd never become too starstruck with them, her psychology background giving her insight into their humanity. But, at the same time – she'd always assumed they were mostly content. After all, why wouldn't they be content? They didn't have someone they thought was a friend betraying them. What did the Bible say about that, she wondered. What does the Bible say to do when your closest friend, perhaps your only friend in the whole world stabs you in the back?

Was it possible to still be happy when you don't get the job – or it gets stolen from you – or if you don't have the money? What about when your wife dies? She thought of Luke again. How tragic a story it was the Rachel had died so young and so in love. How can he be content after that? Why wouldn't God have stopped it? Rachel was a Christian and she loved God. Why would he want her to die? What was it that Joe said? "He could take everything away —and though it might be tougher to swallow, I know it would be the best thing for me." Was having her career taken away the best thing for her?

Around and around her thoughts went. Luke, God, Anna, Ruth, Minden, St. Louis, Millennium, Byte, Anna, Joe, Luke.

When she spent too long thinking about it, her anger at Anna wore off and all that remained was sadness. It had broken her heart to lose her friend. They started at Millennium at the same time and even lived together for a couple years when they were low-level staffers with mountains of student loans to pay off. Neither of them dated often, too busy with work. They took weekend trips together— to Nashville or Chicago. Shopping, eating, dancing. Where had it all gone wrong? Why didn't Anna care about Charlotte the way Charlotte cared about her? Not for the first time in her life, Charlotte wondered if it was her that was broken and unlovable.

By the time dinner rolled around, she was exhausted, even though she'd done nothing all day but go to church, sit on the porch, or pace her beloved cottage. She fixed her favorite comfort food —a grilled cheese sandwich—grabbed a book, and collapsed in bed; determined to shut out her thoughts for at least an hour or two before falling asleep.

~

LUKE'S DAY WAS DIFFERENT. After church, he promised Todd he would come help build a retaining wall. This wasn't a paying gig, except in the common male tradition that pizza plus beer could always be traded for manual labor. Luke was glad for the activity and for the company. He became friends with Todd shortly after moving to Minden. Todd had graduated high school with Rachel and was one of her closest friends. Todd was quick to adopt Luke into his circle. Being one of the few young locals who didn't go off to college meant that Todd knew everyone in town and that every one knew Todd.

They shoveled the slope of earth out and hauled block from the pickup bed to line up where Todd wanted the ridge of the wall to be. It was warm, and they both removed their shirts before long.

"I haven't seen Charlotte around lately, did you finally chase her off like you wanted to from the beginning?" Todd knew the story behind Luke's aversion to Charlotte living at the cabin. He also knew that Miss Ruth had laid her foot down and forced the issue. After their evening at the bar when Luke and Charlotte had walked out together with what appeared to be an old friend, Todd hadn't seen her around.

"She's still here. Even came to church this morning." Luke wasn't sure why he needed to share that, almost to defend Charlotte. But from what? "She seems to be settling in. I think she likes it here."

"Do you want her to like it here?" It was easy to see that Luke was struggling with his feelings for the pretty woman from St. Louis and Todd desperately wanted to see if he would admit them. "Wouldn't it be easier if she hated it?"

Luke nodded. "Yep, that sure would've been easier. But... I don't know, Todd. I think she needs to be here. I think... I think God brought her here." Luke wasn't sure if he sounded as crazy as he felt saying that out loud. "I still hate the thought of someone else living in our cabin, but I guess I think Rachel would like her, and she'd probably kick my butt for how I treated her when she first showed up." Luke smiled at the thought. Rachel would have been appalled at his lack of hospitality. She was, after all, the most welcoming person Luke had ever met—besides Ruth, who undoubtedly passed that trait on to her daughter. He continued. "She's not so bad, once you get to know her a bit. We talked a lot at the bar the other night and I think I understand her a bit better. I think she understands me a bit more, too."

Not that Luke understood himself much at all. Had he really called her sweetheart? When she had pointed that out, his heart sank and he felt immeasurably guilty. It's not that he had forgotten about Rachel—no, he would never forget about Rachel. What was it that made him call Charlotte by the endearment he only used for his wife?

Luke sighed. "I don't know, Todd. I like her, ya know? I want to ruffle her feathers, make her laugh. Loosen her up. But maybe she's not capable of it." *Maybe she just doesn't like me.*

Todd grinned. "I know what you mean. She relaxes a little bit and lets her guard down, and then it is up again in a hurry. I caught that the couple of times we've been out together."

Luke considered this. "Exactly." They worked in silence for a while before Luke spoke again. "She's not a believer."

Todd nodded, "Yeah. I figured."

"How can I feel this way about someone who doesn't share our faith? What do I do about it."

"Just be patient, Luke. It'll all work out how it is supposed to work out, ya know? That's what I keep telling myself about Chrissy."

"Yeah, man. What's up with that? You guys hang out almost every day."

Todd rolled his eyes. "We're just friends. For now."

"Why haven't you made a move."

Todd jerked a shoulder. "I'm waiting for the right time."

With a shake of his head, Luke responded. "Just don't wait so long she finds someone else."

Todd grunted in acknowledgment, effectively shutting down the conversation.

Luke and Todd continued to work in silence and Luke did the only thing he could think to. He prayed. For Charlotte. But also for himself.

SEPTEMBER GAVE way to October and the town began to take on the comforting warmth of fall. Signs for the Annual Harvest Festival popped up, though the event was more than a month away. Patriotic decorations left from the Fourth of July were replaced with cheery pumpkins and 'Thankful' themed signs. Fake cobwebs and decorative bats and spiders adorned some of the shop fronts. Crafty Corner, the craft and yarn store, had transitioned their display window to homemade wreaths, signs, and chunky sweaters and warm weather clothes made from the yarns they sold there.

Next door at The Rolling Pin bakery, the window displayed delicious looking cupcakes with jack-o-lantern tops, pumpkin and leaf-shaped frosted cookies, and beautiful bread braided to look like a sheaf of wheat. The sign advised patrons to order their Thanksgiving pies soon. Charlotte thought about what she would be doing back in St. Louis to celebrate the season, and figured the peak of her festivity would be a pumpkin spiced latte from the chain coffee shop she often frequented. She mentioned the craving for that seasonal specialty to Chrissy in passing.

A week later, when she stopped by the cafe for a chat, Chrissy surprised her by making the sweet and spiced drink. Chrissy found out that the flavoring was available from their coffee vendor and added some to their next order. Charlotte was nearly moved to tears. She knew it was a small thing, but she'd never really had friends that would have gone out of their way to do something nice for her. Not even Anna, who had been her closest friend for years would have remembered the comment and made it happen, just because.

"It's no big deal, Charlotte," Chrissy insisted. "I like pumpkin spice too! Besides, I want to try serving more of this type of stuff here. Bring us in to the 21st century!"

Charlotte sipped her drink, and tried her best not to end up with whipped cream on her nose. "Well, thanks again. It officially feels like fall now."

"It sure does. Isn't Minden just the perfect place, so safe and cozy? We'll have a few more warm spells, I bet. But for the most part, I think Fall is here to stay."

Charlotte's recruiter radar flashed on the word *safe*. There was something in Chrissy's past making her cling to the security of Minden and the cafe. But what?

Charlotte rolled the rest of Chrissy's comment over in her mind. *Here to stay. Here to stay.* Fall might be here to stay, but was she? Would she see autumn fade into winter here? What about Spring? She'd initially planned to be here for a year. So much could happen in one year though. Charlotte tried to picture October of next year. But she wasn't holding a pumpkin spice latte walking through the streets of St. Louis in her designer coat and high-heeled boots. She saw herself, passing mashed potatoes to Luke around Miss Ruth's table, while he joked about saving room for pie.

She pictured herself having a chat with Chrissy over a latte served in a real ceramic mug like the one she held now. When she pictured fall next year, it was the falling leaves of the woods, in their brilliant red, orange, and yellow hues she saw. The longer she stayed in Minden, the more it felt like she never wanted to leave. The people here were special. There was something different about how people treated each other. Despite their hardships, her friends from Minden were content. They didn't seem to crave the important job titles or country club memberships she'd been conditioned to strive for. The more she thought about it, she figured it wasn't a small town versus the city thing. Charlotte grew up in a small town and she remembered the blanket of depression, self-pity, and bitterness covering her parents and the other adults she knew then. She tried to put her finger on what was missing as she compared the two experiences.

Charlotte sought Luke out a few days later, finally finding him caring for the potted mums that now lined Main Street, giving the street a distinct feel of autumn. "I want it, Luke."

"Want it?" Luke looked confused. Not surprising, given her non sequitur.

"I want contentment. Peace. Joy. I want to trust that even when my plans don't work out God has better ones in store. I want to be as sure about my purpose in life as you are. I want to not care that I got fired. I want to not care that my friend betrayed me. I want it to stop hurting. I want to trust people again." She was standing next to him now, looking the opposite way. The words came out as an uninterrupted stream of consciousness, pouring over from her thoughts of the last few days. Charlotte caught her breath and waited for Luke to respond, afraid to look at him after her confession.

Luke's face softened. "Oh, sweetheart. God can give you contentment, and peace and joy and purpose. Trusting him won't make you not care, though. Hurts will still sting. Betrayals will still cut you open. It will still be painful when your dreams don't come true. But you'll have the best healer to mend the scars. And you'll have something bigger than all of those to lean on when it does hurt." He stood up, removed his gloves, and took her hands in his. "Come on. I'll buy you lunch and we can talk."

They drove to Greencastle, a town about twenty minutes away so they could eat and talk without seeing everyone in town. Conversation was stilted on the way, and Luke prayed fervently the whole trip. *Father, Abba, I've never done this before. Please give me the words to say. Please don't let me screw this up. Help me show her who You are. How much You love her. What if I don't have answers to the questions she asks? What if this is too soon and she's not ready? Father, you are in control. Speak to Charlotte through me.*

Once they had ordered and were waiting for their food, Charlotte wasted no time. "How do I get it, Luke? How do I get the contentment the pastor was talking about?"

Luke smiled. "It's pretty simple, but there is some ground we need to cover first. What do you know about Jesus?"

During their lunch, Luke answered all her questions. She had a million. They talked about the need for forgiveness and Jesus' victory on the cross. She made the connection to Christmas and questioned the evil in the world despite a loving God. He walked her through asking God into her heart and life and felt the Spirit move as though it was his own redemptive prayer again. *This is the coolest thing I've ever been a part of. Thank you for choosing me, Father.*

Before he dropped her off at her car, he asked to pray with her again. "You are a good, good Father. You brought Charlotte here, out of the city and into this place to encounter You. Thank you for your perfect plan and your endless love. As Charlotte grows in her faith in You, make your presence known, Father. You have promised us in the book of Matthew, 'seek, and we shall find.' We know that we should never stop seeking you, Lord, and that you will continue to reveal yourself to us. Thank you, thank you, thank you, kind Father."

"How do you do that?" Charlotte asked when he had finished.

"Do what?"

"Pray. How do you do it?" Matter of fact, Charlotte asked the question. Any pretense she held of having all the answers had been knocked down over lunch and the endless questions she'd already asked.

"You can do it too, Charlotte. Just talk to God. He loves you. He wants to hear from you. Just talk to him. Most of my prayers aren't out loud, and a few of them are even written down. There is no right way or wrong way to do it. We are told to 'pray without ceasing.' Treat God like your best friend, and talk to him whenever you want."

"Thanks, Luke. I've never felt like this before. So... happy, I guess!" She laughed, a ringing melodic sound that had his heart singing in response. "I had a career, friends, money. But it never made me feel like this. Thank you." She leaned over and gave him an awkward hug while he was still restrained by the seatbelt.

Luke gave a short squeeze and relished the contact. Then, he shook his head and looked her in the eyes. "I didn't do anything, sweetheart. God did it, and you let Him." Luke needed her to understand. This wasn't something he had done. It was all Jesus.

LUKE RACED to Ruth's house, eager to share the news with her. It wasn't until halfway through the door he realized maybe it wasn't his news to share. As he stood in the hallway, trying to decide how to proceed, Charlotte came running in the door behind him, with a joyful cry of Ruth's name already escaping her lips.

She let her the cry die, and released a loud laugh in its place. Her wide smile took his breath away. *Now isn't that a most beautiful sound...* Luke laughed with her, and Miss Ruth came walking down the hallway toward them.

"What's all this now? How's a woman to get any rest around here?" Ruth spoke with a smile, her tone almost teasing.

Luke glanced at Charlotte and gestured for her to explain.

Charlotte bounced on her toes as the news burst out. "I became a Christian, Miss Ruth. I believe!"

Miss Ruth let out a squeal that would be envied by a teenage girl and flew into Charlotte's arms. "Oh, thank you, Lord. So good," she murmured into Charlotte's hair as they embraced. Luke felt as though he were intruding on the emotional moment, but he couldn't tear himself away. It felt so right to be here, celebrating with Ruth and Charlotte.

Luke had a realization, and then turned to Ruth. "Mom, I know you have an extra Bible laying around here somewhere. Do you have one we could give Charlotte?"

Miss Ruth opened her eyes and moved quickly. "Oh yes, of course I do. Of course! Let's step into the library and I'll grab one."

After they filed in, Ruth reached for a shelf and began to speak again, her voice soft and reverent. "I know just the one I'd like you to have." She pulled out a purple soft-bound book, an inch and a half thick. The edges of the cover were bent, and there were papers sticking out from inside. She handed it to Charlotte, and gave a worried glance to Luke. He caught her eyes and saw the questions there. Then he looked again at the Bible now being caressed by Charlotte's manicured fingers.

Is that... Rachel's Bible? I can't believe I never wondered what happened to it. Luke was filled with sweet memories of Rachel pouring over the words of that book, showing him verses and teaching him. He expected guilt but it didn't come. Luke had the overwhelming reassurance that Rachel's Bible was waiting all this time for the perfect home. *Rachel would approve.* He smiled at Ruth because this felt right. Ruth's eyes shined with moisture and she gave him a grateful nod.

"I think this one will be perfect for you, Charlotte." Ruth's voice was warm and approving.

Charlotte looked up from the soft leather, where she traced the gilded letters with her fingers. "Thank you so much, Miss Ruth. I can't wait to read it."

Ruth didn't say anything to Charlotte about the Bible's previous owner; so neither did he.

All three of them celebrated that night and when Miss Ruth went up to bed, Luke and Charlotte walked outside into the still, dark night. The cicadas drone was loud, and the chirp from the crickets punctuated the buzz with a melody. "Care to take a walk with me?" Luke asked gently, extending his hand toward her.

"Of course." Charlotte took his hand and he led them toward the gardens.

Luke asked, "Have you spent much time out here?" In response, Charlotte shook her head. "These gardens were how I earned my keep when I first moved here." He laughed. "Of course, they expand every year. I could landscape this entire forest and never feel I've repaid Ruth for everything she's given me."

Charlotte looked at the spread of greenery laid before them. "I love it. I remember the first day Todd brought me here and I saw the gardens." The path wound through the front yard, twisting and turning around trees and bushes. Forks in the path led to secluded nooks with benches and fountains and bird baths. "How do you maintain it?"

"I prefer to do it myself, but sometimes I catch Ruth out here weeding or splitting bulbs." Luke shook her head and rolled his eyes. "I know she enjoys gardening, but it would be overwhelming to do herself. Usually, I send someone from the crew out if I can't get to it." Luke hated having to do that, but at least it was still his designs and his gift to Ruth.

Whatever walls had been there between her and Luke had been torn down during the day's events. She asked another question. Charlotte wanted to know everything. "Tell me about your business. How did you come to own your own?"

"Well, I told you I worked as a landscaper at Indiana University when I met Rachel, right?" Charlotte nodded in the dark. "When I came up here, I didn't have any other skills. I felt so terrible about mooching off Ruth and Rachel that Ruth came up with a way for me to earn my keep. She told me she had always dreamt of having a garden to walk in and enjoy the flowers, right here at the house. She gave me a budget, and let me figure out the rest. It was my very first project." He smiled, remembering. "Looking back now, the very first beds I did were terrible. The beds had tall flowers in the front, blocking the shorter ones. They had flowers that require full sun stuck in places with all shade. I've pretty much redone all of that first attempt by now. But it felt so good to do it. I started studying horticulture and landscape design. Rachel and I took road trips to the Indianapolis Museum of Art where they have acres and acres of beautiful gardens. I got hired by others to do more basic work – mowing grass, planting trees, mulching existing beds. Eventually, others gave me a chance to do true landscaping, and I fixed Ruth's gardens enough that people saw what I could do. I officially started my own business around a year after that first Thanksgiving with Ruth and Rachel." Then, he added something and Charlotte saw his heart in the words. "God has blessed it and made it successful."

How many men and women Charlotte knew would never give credit to anyone but themselves for their success. But Luke gave glory to God in everything. Even the business he built with his own two hands and backbreaking work.

They wound their way to the back of the house, and passed under a trellis. Big purple and white clematis flowering ivy climbed to the top, where Luke knew they would be seeking the sun in the heat of the day. Luke didn't notice Charlotte had stopped until he felt the tug on his hand where it joined hers. He turned back and she stepped closer to him.

She tilted her head to look up at him"You are pretty incredible. You know that, Mr. Brand?"

Luke blushed and was grateful for the dark. Knowing he couldn't resist any longer, he leaned down and kissed her. She lifted her head to him and stepped into his embrace. His hand continued to hold hers, and his other came up to circle her small waist. In that moment, nothing else existed. As the kiss deepened, Charlotte's hand suddenly came up and Luke heard a 'smack' sound near his face and felt the whoosh of air. When he broke the kiss, he caught Charlotte's sheepish smile as she swatted another mosquito from her forehead.

"It seems we have a million tiny chaperones," he joked.

"Yeah, and they are relentless." She looked at him, and he heard the reluctance in her voice. *She doesn't want the night to end! Good... Neither do I.* The day had been a whirlwind of heavy conversations and light-hearted celebrations. But it had been a life changing day for Charlotte. And for him, he realized. He knew they needed to head in for the night, though.

He vocalized that thought and began leading Charlotte toward the cabin. "Charlotte?" At her name, she looked at him, waiting. "Would you spend next Saturday with me?"

She smiled broadly and his heart soared. "I'd love to."

15

———

The next morning, Charlotte opened up her eyes with a smile. Thoughts of the wonderful day, and night, before with Luke flooded her. *Well, God. Luke said to talk to you like a best friend, so here it goes. Last night was amazing. Luke is just incredible. Thank you for bringing me to him. Thanks for everything, I guess. This feels weird. How do I know you can hear me?*

Despite her solitude, she felt self-conscious and silly holding a one-sided conversation. But she didn't stop trying. Throughout the week, she devoured the words within her new Bible with the help of Ruth. And with the help of previous owner, who had left passages underlined and highlighted. Hand-written notes decorated the margins. When she texted something that caught her eye, Luke responded with something she didn't know about it or a different verse of his own. He started sending her a verse every day, a mini-treasure hunt for her to track down by book and chapter of the unfamiliar book. And she kept trying to talk to God.

Charlotte felt like a character in a teen movie, her heels kicked in the air as she talked to her boyfriend on the phone until the late hours of the night. Her teenage years had never included anything so carefree. She hadn't seen Luke since the walk in the garden. So unlike her feelings when she'd first arrived in Minden, Charlotte missed him.

"What did you do today?" she asked, staring up at the wood plank ceiling above the bed where she laid on the phone.

Luke yawned. It was after eleven, she realized with a quick glance of her phone. "I went to the office early and did a bunch of paperwork before my crew arrived. We had a big job in Terre Haute, and then when we got back I needed to get the leaves under control at the church. I got home about nine." He groaned. "I'm exhausted. But I keep telling myself it will be worth it when I get to take the entire day off on Saturday to spend with you." Charlotte warmed at his words and stifled her grin in the nearby pillow.

LUKE HADN'T LIED. He was exhausted. Long days getting ahead on his biggest ongoing project and late nights on the phone with Charlotte were catching up to him. He smiled remembering some of their conversations. They had grilled each other on everything – favorite color (both green), favorite foods (sushi – *yuck!* – and ribs), biggest fear (spiders and heights). And they had talked about God, a lot. Luke was in awe of Charlotte's curiosity and insight. She asked questions and challenged him, but he loved sharing with her what he knew. He was excited for their day together. Whenever Charlotte felt flustered or jumped to conclusions, he thought back to the day she went hiking in teeny-tiny shorts and refused to listen to him. Luke remembered waiting for her so he knew she wasn't lost. Then, he had bailed, not wanting to deal with the fallout of her hike. That day, the temptation to leave her a note inviting her to see his favorite places in the woods had been strong, but he had chickened out. Even then, when he hadn't accepted her moving in to the cabin and was still struggling with his own ability to let go; he wanted to accompany Charlotte on that hike. And today he was going to.

Luke texted her with a "Good morning, beautiful" message and told her she should wear long pants and tennis shoes about an hour before he was due to meet her at the cabin. He spent that time getting ready himself and loading a backpack with bottles of water and some things for a light lunch. He intended to show Charlotte his favorite place in the woods, and it was quite a hike. Luke didn't want hunger to force an end to their special day.

Charlotte smiled broadly at him when he arrived, and Luke couldn't help but return the grin. He resisted the urge to make a teasing comment about her long pants. Luke had to admit, he missed the shorts.

Charlotte gave him a quick hug and then pulled on the edges of her jacket. "I didn't know whether short sleeves were okay, so I wore a tank top under a jacket? Does that work?"

"That's perfect. We're hiking and it's a little chilly now, but it won't be for long. You should be able to hike in your tank top once the sun is a bit further overhead. Here, I brought this for you, too."

He handed her a container of bug spray from the side pocket of the backpack with a smile.

Charlotte attempted to make an angry face, but couldn't pull it off. She admitted to the mosquito bites after her previous hike on one of their phone calls. She laughed instead and said, "Thanks, Luke. I totally forgot and I really don't want a repeat of last time."

"Neither do I. Your skin is too pretty to mar with bug bites." Luke watched, distracted, as a hint of color rose on her cheeks. Then, he cleared his throat. "Let's get going. We've got a long hike ahead of us." Luke found the familiar trail a few steps beyond the treeline. Charlotte was grateful he was leading the way. Last time she'd been out here, she had practically wandered in circles for twenty-five minutes before finding her way back to the cottage. Stubbornly, Charlotte would never admit it, but a rising anxiety that she'd never find her way back had threatened to take over at the time. She admitted that was a terribly pessimistic thought after twenty-five minutes of hiking.

Charlotte followed Luke through the woods, carefully avoiding the protruding roots he was diligent to point out to her, and following his extended index finger with her eyes and spotting the bright red cardinal perched on a tree to their left.

After about an hour, Luke sat down on a large fallen log and pulled out a bottle of water and handed it to her. While they both guzzled down the cool water, Charlotte studied him. Small beads of swear had formed on his brow and he wiped his forehead with the sleeve of his t-shirt by lifting his arm across his face. Luke caught her staring and smiled at her when she blushed. "We are about halfway there."

"Seriously, only halfway?" Charlotte felt like they'd been hiking for hours. She ignored the protests of her thighs as she stood up from the log.

"It'll be worth it, I promise." Luke gave her a wink and she knew she'd follow him until the soles of her shoes wore out.

"It better be, buster," she joke. Even if the destination was just another log like this, she'd be content. The first hour hiking had been mostly silent. To Charlotte, it had almost felt like disturbing the morning to do anything other than soak in the sounds of the woods coming to life and the sun rising to a place of prominence above the trees. Now, though, Charlotte removed her light jacket, and carried the water bottle with her. She and Luke fell into a natural rhythm of conversation with valleys of silence.

"Isn't it beautiful out here?" she asked.

"I love these woods," Luke agreed. "Ruth owns a lot of them, but there is another family that owns the rest. I hope no one ever decides to get rid of it. There aren't a lot of woods like these left."

The second half of their hike flew by, and Charlotte suspected Luke had scheduled their first break a little further into the hike than halfway. Luke stopped at some landmark she wouldn't recognize, and then guided her to a small ridge to their left side. When Charlotte could see over the hill, she realized what she'd been hearing for the last hundred yards or so. A formation of rocks cascaded down the hillside. They stood on a ridge off to the side of it and could see a stream flow from the valley of two hills onto the rocks below, pooling in shallow pools before cascading down rocks in multiple avenues. The entire formation was ten feet high and ten feet across, but it extended nearly thirty feet from the top to the lowest basin further down the stream.

Luke watched Charlotte take in the waterfall and enjoyed as she followed the water from the top through the various levels of rocks and pools down each path of the falls. When it rained on Thursday night, he knew exactly where he wanted to bring Charlotte today. It was beautiful when dry, too and you could climb up the rocks and sit in the crevices under the overhangs of shale. But, when the water flowed from the surrounding hills and the runoff caught the flash of light through the trees beginning to drop their leaves; it was a magical place.

"Wow," Charlotte practically breathed the word, hesitant to break the spell. "It's amazing. I never would have guessed it was here! No one ever said anything."

Luke spoke softly, matching her volume and reverence. "It's my little secret. Rachel and I found it one day years ago... I've come back here a few times after she died. I guess I find it a good place to think. It reminds me that God is the creator of beauty and balance. And that all the other garbage in the world isn't really that important after all."

Unable to disagree, Charlotte nodded and stared back out over the waterfall, listening to the steady flow of water falling on rock and water.

They hiked down the ridge, along the falls until they stood at the base of it, on a large smooth rock. Luke set down the backpack and sat with his legs hanging over the edge. When Charlotte sat too, still unable to look away from the falls, he elbowed her. "Hey. You hungry?"

At the mundane question, Charlotte seemed to wake up. She thought about it and replied casually, "I could eat." However, her attempt to play it cool was thwarted by the sudden gurgle of her stomach beneath her tank top – loud enough to be heard even over the droning of the waterfall.

Luke threw his head back and laughed, while Charlotte admitted sheepishly, "I might be really hungry."

"Well, then I guess it is a good thing I brought sustenance." He grabbed the backpack and pulled out a small cooler. "I've got peanut butter and jelly, a couple apples, some cheese sticks, and some pretzels. What do you want first?"

"I don't remember the last time I had a peanut butter and jelly sandwich." She reached for it and then, pulled her hand back. "Wait, what kind of jelly is it?"

"Strawberry." Luke answered, amused, and wondering where this was going.

"Oh good," she explained as she unwrapped the now accepted sandwich. "Grape and strawberry are the only kinds I'll eat. My mom always used to make us eat apricot and orange jelly and I hated it!"

Luke laughed, "I didn't know one could have such strong feelings about jelly. It's just a condiment. Not like I put bananas on them."

"Oh my gosh, peanut butter and banana sandwiches are the best thing ever!"

He gave an exaggerated gag. "That's disgusting."

"Have you ever tried it?" she insisted.

He shook his head firmly. "I don't have to try sushi to know I don't like it."

After a bite of sandwich, she leaned into him with a nudge. "Don't even get me started on your sushi hang-up mister. We are going to educate you in the wonderful culinary experience that is sushi."

"Whatever you say, sweetheart." Luke still had no plans of letting raw fish enter his mouth, but he did like the assumption that they would be having another date. Many more dates, if he had anything to say about it.

They ate their apples and threw the cores into the woods to see who could throw it the furthest – Luke did, but Charlotte insisted it was only because hers hit a tree five feet in front of them. Then, they took off their shoes and waded in the creek. The water was cold, numbing her toes against the rocks, but was only a few inches deep in any one spot. Charlotte climbed to the first tier of rocks above the bottom basin, and Luke was right behind her, making sure she didn't slip. She turned around, her chin slightly above his nose and looked down at him.

"So this is what it's like," she stated matter of factly.

"What what's like?"

"Kissing someone shorter than you." And then she leaned over and did just that.

Surprised for only a moment, Luke gladly tipped his head up to meet her kiss and then grabbed her around the waist and hauled her back down to his level. Charlotte laughed and then reached down behind her into the water where she had been standing, and splashed Luke right in the chest and neck.

He sputtered and caught her when she tried to slip away down the creek bed. "I don't think so, sweetheart." He rubbed his cold, wet neck all over hers. Gradually, his playful nuzzling turned heated as he smelled her light perfume, still sweet and fragrant behind her ears, despite the morning heat. He laid a kiss there and it trailed to where the throb of her heartbeat lived at the base of her neck. Her hands clutched at his shirt, and her head hung back to allow him easier access. Luke skimmed his hands from where they rested on her hips along her ribcage and then back down again.

Luke's lips found hers again. This kiss was hot and hungry as he pulled her waist to his, loving the feel of her entire body against his. He groaned into her and backed away inch by inch, missing the warmth of her but needing the space to collect his thoughts.

Charlotte breathed heavily. "Whoa."

Luke only nodded in agreement, his eyes shifting between staring at her, staring at his hands, and closing in what looked to Charlotte very much like pain. "You can't imagine what you do to me, Charlotte Walters."

I bet I can, Charlotte thought wryly, thinking of the way she had offered herself to him for the taking.

"Come on, let's head back to the house." Luke had to say something and distract them both, or he would end up tugging her back into his arms for a repeat performance.

The entire way back, Luke replayed that kiss—that more-than-a-kiss—he corrected and prayed for wisdom and strength. Charlotte was a new Christian, after all. It was his responsibility to be the accountable one. Luke didn't exactly feel guilty about what had happened as much as he recognized how close to the slippery line in the sand they had come. And how easy and tempting it would be to go too far with this woman, too quickly.

Charlotte picked up on the tension in the air after the kiss, easily reading it all over Luke's facial expressions and body language. She did her best to lighten the mood on their hike back to the house, teasing him about being a slave driver and quizzing him about his favorite movies.

"Do we have plans after we get back?" She was hoping the day with him wouldn't be over when the hike was. If that was the case, Charlotte figured she would start walking a lot slower.

Luke looked back at her from his place a few steps ahead on the trail. "Well, I figured we could both take some time to clean up and rest and then maybe we would go have dinner?" Charlotte couldn't stop the smile from spreading across her cheeks. She bit her lip and nodded.

"Yeah, dinner sounds good."

RUTH WAS PULLING weeds when she heard Luke and Charlotte return from their hike. She was overjoyed that Charlotte was finally beginning to recognize why she had been brought to Minden. Yet, she worried constantly about Luke's growing attachment to the young woman. In every conversation Charlotte and Ruth had, Charlotte always indicated the intention of returning to the city, repairing her reputation and reviving her broken career. *I just don't see how this can work. Luke will be heartbroken when she leaves. I've seen him hurt enough.* Memories of that night at the hospital flooded her.

Rachel looked impossibly small lying in the hospital bed. Surrounded by machines; cables and tubes snaked their way along Rachel's arms and cheeks. The ventilator made a rhythmic whoosh every few seconds as it forced air into her lungs, and the heart monitor beeped a steady beat. Her face was pale and bruised and bandages covered her scalp where they had shaved her pretty long hair to perform the surgery.

The doctors explained Rachel's condition to them. The accident damaged most of her internal organs, and much of the damage was irreparable. It also caused what the doctor called a "placental abruption." At those words, Ruth cried out and fell into the closest chair while Luke looked on in pained confusion. The doctor elaborated, "I'm so sorry. Your wife was pregnant. About three months along. There was nothing we could do to save the baby. Unfortunately, your wife's injuries are too severe, also. Even with the ventilator, she won't survive for long. There was just too much damage to her liver, lungs, and spleen. You can stay with her until she goes. Again, I'm incredibly sorry for your loss."

Ruth watched, helpless, as Luke struggled through the anger and raw pain of the current tragedy. He clenched his fists and when he couldn't find something to swing at, he pressed his fingers to wet, bloodshot eyes. Luke collapsed against the wall, slid to the floor and pounded the floor with a closed fist. "No, no, no. Not Rachel... a baby... my family" His disoriented pleas cut through Ruth's own grief. Rachel was her baby, after all. Ruth had said goodbye to her husband over a decade ago. But that was different - they had time to process, to talk and laugh and reminisce. This awful reality was too sudden. She wouldn't get to hear her baby laugh again, or watch her become a mother alongside Luke, the man she loved so much. Luke, who was pulling himself up to sit at Rachel's side, just as he'd been since they arrived several hours ago, waiting for an update. Praying for a miracle.

Ruth sat in one corner of the room, with silent tears running down her cheeks as she contemplated saying goodbye to her precious little girl. Luke held

Rachel's limp hand and laid his forehead on the bed next to her arm. Deep, racking sobs shook through him. He looked over at Ruth. "Did you know?" he choked out the words in anguish. "Did you know she was... pregnant?"

Ruth just shook her head. Rachel had kept the secret from both of them. The grandchild Ruth would never have, and the son or daughter that Luke would never hold.

Luke walked up from the cabin, pulling Ruth from her memory and back to the flower beds she was weeding. He bent down and kissed Ruth on the cheek, rubbing a bit of extra sweat on her to hear her laugh. Moving past the tears that threatened to escape, she did laugh and swatted at him with her gardening glove.

"You know I could have one of my guys do that, Mom." He'd told her a thousand times not to work so hard, especially in the heat of the day.

"It's just a few weeds, child, and I'm perfectly capable of helping care for this beautiful garden. Did you and Charlotte have fun today?"

Luke smiled, remembering exactly how much fun they'd had. "We had a great time."

Ruth looked back down at the dirt, considering her next words carefully. "I don't want you to get hurt, Lucas. What happens when she leaves and goes back to St. Louis?"

Luke shook his head. "I don't know, Mom, but I have a feeling it's all going to work out."

Ruth continued, ignoring his words. "I love Charlotte, but she's going to break your heart."

"I don't think so, Mom. Not at all." And he didn't. He could no longer picture Minden without Charlotte. Even though he'd never heard her say she was staying for good, he couldn't imagine her wanting to leave the town he loved so much. She had to love it too, right? What was there not to love?

Ruth just gave him a forced smile and stood up. "I hope you're right. I really do. I'll be praying about it."

"Thanks, Mom." And with that settled, Luke walked back down to his truck and began looking forward to the remainder of his day with Charlotte. There was nothing that could bring him down today.

16

During another late night phone call, Charlotte admitted to Luke that she'd never carved a pumpkin. He was shocked. Even with his lackluster example of a mother, he'd carved pumpkins. The next night, he showed up at the cabin with a giant pumpkin in one hand and a toolbox in the other. Charlotte greeted him with a grin and grabbed the toolbox from him as she let him inside. "What did you do? I thought we were meeting up with the gang at Bulldogs?"

Luke explained as he set the pumpkin on the counter. "I told them we couldn't make it. I can't have my girlfriend ignorant in the art of pumpkin carving." He looked at her, suddenly a little unsure of himself, "Is that okay? We can still go, if you'd rather not do this."

Charlotte reassured him, "This is great, seriously. Thank you."

Luke ducked back out to his truck to grab the second pumpkin and Charlotte opened the small toolbox. With raised eyebrows, she took in the knives of different sizes, a big metal serving spoon, several nails, and a hodgepodge of markers, tape, candles, and lighters. Intimidated already, she closed the toolbox quickly and sat on the barstool. Luke came back in with another huge pumpkin and a stack of newspapers. While she watched, he covered the countertop with the newspaper and grabbed a big knife.

"Okay, first things first. We need to empty out the inside of the pumpkin. It gets kind of messy," he added, gesturing to the newspapers. After the stem had been cut from the pumpkin, he pulled her from her perch on the stool and stood her in front of the pumpkin. "Dig in, sweetheart."

Charlotte lifted onto her tiptoes and peered into the pumpkin. The stringy mess of pulp and seeds greeted her. "Umm, what?"

Luke smiled and tried to cover his chuckle. "Dig in. We've got to get all of that," he pointed to the pulp, and then to the counter, "out. Just plop it all on the newspaper." He grabbed a sheet pan from the drawer under the stove, "Then we will sort out the seeds."

Charlotte still hadn't done anything. She looked at the pumpkin and back at Luke again. And back to the pumpkin. One more look at Luke's excited face and she sighed. "Do I have to use my hands?"

Luke just got a goofy grin and nodded. The mix of curiosity and disgust on Charlotte's face was endlessly entertaining. As he watched and tried not to snicker, the look changed from disgust to determination. Charlotte lowered her hand into the slimy mess, coming back up with a good-sized handful of the pulp and seeds. It was entertaining to see Charlotte out of her element. But he was also proud of her. The woman wasn't afraid of anything. While she continued letting handfuls of pulp splat on the newspaper, Luke cut the top off the second pumpkin and began cleaning it out. When it was nearly empty, he grabbed the large metal spoon from the toolbox and got the last bits still clinging to the walls of the pumpkin.

Charlotte, noticing his tool, suddenly spoke up, "What?! I could have used that spoon this whole time? My fingernails are filled with this nasty orange goo from trying to scrape it all from the edges. Lucas Brand, you are in big trouble!" The laughter in her voice gave away her false indignation. With a laugh, Luke knocked the last bit of pulp from his spoon and handed it to her. "Well, I don't need it now – I'm all done." She gasped and narrowed her eyes at him. Then, Charlotte shocked both of them by wiping her slimy pumpkin hands all over his shirt before running away, laughing maniacally.

Luke gaped in the direction she had run, unwilling to believe prim and proper Charlotte Walters had just slimed him. Unable to hold it in, he started laughing as well and followed her.

Charlotte had shut herself in the bedroom. "Come on, Charlotte. You can come out!" He rapped a clean knuckle on the solid door.

"Not a chance," she called. "I know you, Luke. Go wash your hands first!" He stifled a laugh in his shoulder and then looked at his slimy hands. Hands he'd rolled through the pulpy mess after she'd slimed him, intentionally getting them as gross as possible.

"You wound me!" He said, dramatically. "What kind of man do you think I am?"

Again, her playful voice called through the door. "Go wash your hands!" Luke stepped into the hallway bathroom and let her hear him wash his hands.

"Okay, all clean. Happy?" A brief pause told him she was considering the situation. The door cracked open and he saw the laughter in Charlotte's eyes as she looked for his hands. Luke held them out for inspection. "Satisfied? Now can we go finish?"

Charlotte's eyes moved toward the kitchen, but instead of opening the door, she pursed her lips to hide a smile. "You've got to get rid of all the slime. Then I'll come out."

Luke rolled his eyes, but went back to the kitchen. He sorted out enough pumpkin seeds to roast for a snack and discarded the rest of the pulp before calling the all clear signal with a laugh.

Charlotte approached him cautiously, but Luke just shook his head. From his back pocket, he pulled out printed sheets with intricate designs. "Here. I found some designs for us to choose from. What do you want on your pumpkin?"

Apparently, there was an art to the craft she had never appreciated, because none of the designs were the standard "jack-o-lantern" she was expecting. Leafing through the papers, Charlotte landed on one that seemed fairly simple – a pretty collection of autumn leaves.

Luke taped the paper to the pumpkin and she watched as he showed her how to trace the pattern onto the pumpkin by poking holes through the paper with a nail. After she had traced each leaf with nail holes, he reluctantly held out a knife. He pulled it away as she reached for it.

"Carve away from your body and keep your other hand far away,' he lectured. Charlotte rolled her eyes at his lack of confidence in her and grabbed the knife handle. She started cutting. It felt a bit like connect-the-dots from kindergarten, but infinitely harder. After her knife slipped the first time, narrowly missing her left hand, she appreciated Luke's pointers.

Much to her dismay, Luke wouldn't let her see his pumpkin until it was completely finished. When he finally revealed it, she was delighted to see the St. Louis Cardinals logo with the familiar Arch over it. Charlotte missed the city, but being here in their small town with Luke was better than she would have ever imagined a month or two ago. While she finished her pumpkin, Luke toasted the pumpkin seeds in the oven with some oil and seasoned salt he had to grab from Ruth's house.

At the end of the night, they sat on the porch chairs and munched the salty snack. The warm glow of the tealights inside the pumpkins revealed the designs in the darkness. It was as perfect a night as Charlotte could ever remember, filled with a contentment and peace that she hadn't known since her grandmother had died. When she said as much to Luke, he simply replied, "I don't know much about your childhood, you know."

Softly, she replied, "I know. I don't tell people much about it." Her past was buried deep; shame and fear long covered by pride and ambition, always threatening to dig its way out and marr the life she'd built. Charlotte would rather forget it, pretend it never happened. Charlotte knew enough of Luke's story to know he would understand. That he wouldn't judge her. And sitting there in the dark, Charlotte knew that tonight she'd uncover it and show her dark, painful past with him.

There, in the quiet of the cool fall evening, she told him where she came from. Who she came from.

"My parents would leave me and my sisters with our grandmother for weeks at a time. She never knew when they were coming back. When Grandma died, they simply left us at the house instead." She shook her head, realizing now how messed up it was. "Apparently, when they disappeared, they went to a rundown trailer parked deep in woods. I learned later, they were making drugs and selling them to a dealer."

She hung her head. "On the rare occasions they were home, they were full of lies and false promises. It wasn't long before they started sampling the merchandise and ended up strung out and even more neglectful than before. My older sister left, leaving me and April to fend for ourselves." A harsh laugh escaped. "We were fourteen and sixteen, both working after school and on weekends to put food on the table and buy clothes from the local Goodwill. A couple of times, my parents showed up for a few days, but always left again – usually stealing whatever cash they could find in my wallet." The betrayal of that theft still stuck with her. How unlovable she must be for her own parents to steal the money they'd saved for groceries.

"Of course, we were young. We never realized that someone had to pay for the house. We were evicted and CPS forced us into foster care." Charlotte sniffed. "April and I were separated." There was long pause before she continued. "April didn't fare well in the system. She got depressed and had drugs and alcohol issues of her own. I told the cops where to find our parents and they were arrested. Rumor had it, they would do 10-15 years in state prison, and it was all anyone at school could talk about. April overdosed shortly after she turned fifteen."

Tears escaped and Charlotte wiped them away with the back of her hand. She hadn't cried over her sister in a long time. Charlotte still felt like she had failed April. Charlotte was older and should have protected her. If she had been smarter, or worked harder then they could have stayed together.

Luke saw the pain etched on Charlotte's face, despite the low, flickering light. "It wasn't your fault."

Charlotte squeezed her eyes shut, unwilling to concede her own responsibility for what happened. Later, Charlotte realized the lies and deception from her parents and the experiences with unpredictable foster parents finely tuned her ability to see microexpressions and accurately read people.

Swallowing painfully, Charlotte ignored Luke's comment and continued. "I was determined to do more, to be more. I kept my head down and finished school. The day after graduation, I stole all the cash from my foster parent's house and took a bus to St. Louis." Even then, she'd felt the prick of conscience at her actions, the couple was nice and she'd only been with them for a few months. They had never reported her theft. Years later, she had sent cash and a note with a simple thank you. Charlotte liked to think they understood. "I sent money back a few years later, but I haven't been back since. My parents were released a few years ago, but I can't seem to care." *After all, they never did.* "Maybe all that makes me a horrible person. But now you know." She finished her and felt the silence stretch. She was desperate to know what Luke was thinking. She had been so sure he wouldn't judge her.

Luke sat silently for a while before speaking. "You didn't have to tell me all that." He continued, "I'm glad you did, but I don't ever want you to feel pressured to share if you don't want to."

Charlotte watched him, trying to get a read despite the dim light. "I didn't feel pressured. I wanted to tell you, Luke." *Please, tell me what you think,* she pleaded internally.

Luke leaned toward her, his elbows resting on his knees. He took her hands in his and rubbed her fingers with his. "The more I get to know you, the more I admire you." Luke cleared his throat, his voice full of emotion. "I think you are a miracle, Charlotte Marie Walters. Truly. And I... I had a wonderful time tonight," he finished lamely, leaving too many words unsaid.

17

Charlotte reread the handwritten note for the third time, trying to understand the ramifications. Her mail from St. Louis had finally been forwarded. This simple piece of it had nearly brought her to her knees. Isolated in Minden, Charlotte was blissfully disconnected from the world she left before. She hadn't checked email since she arrived, and she ditched her phone the day she hit the road. Not a single person knew where she was. The handwritten note had been mailed to her home address several weeks ago by her former assistant. It didn't have many details, but said Millennium was being sued by Byte for breach of contract. In the path of Anna's destruction of Charlotte's career—Byte had paid the price. Details of their search had been made public, including the confidential development plan that the candidate would be responsible for after being hired. Charlotte had insisted on seeing it to make sure she could select the best candidate. And there was no way to prove that she hadn't been the one to leak it.

Luke's truck door slammed outside the cottage, and Charlotte hurriedly tucked the open envelope and letter under the bowl of pine cones decorating the coffee table. She tried hard to push the worry and anger from her mind for a precious few hours and prayed he wouldn't noticed anything amiss. Charlotte couldn't tell him. Not after the wonderful weeks they'd had. So, she smoothed her hair and pasted on a smile as she opened the door just as Luke jogged up the steps to pick her up for dinner.

It had only taken a few weeks here for Charlotte to recognize that Main Street was the common thread holding Minden together. Main Street held the bank and both churches, as well as the cafe and the bar and grill. Other shops, like the bakery and the mechanic shop also claimed residence on the quaint street. The city park was tucked at one end, where it appeared most community gatherings took place - including the softball game.

Despite the proximity to the highway, Main

Street remained relatively quiet except for the local traffic. Unless a traveler was willing to venture a few blocks from the highway for food, they mostly stopped at the QuikStop and then continued on their way. Tonight was no different, and Luke and Charlotte walked hand-in-hand down the block. Each held a to-go cup from Chrissy filled with hot cider. The cinnamon and spice lingered on her tongue and the warmth was welcome as the sun disappeared, leaving behind a chilly breeze. Between the cider, Luke's hand in hers, and the coziness of the scarf she'd crocheted; she barely felt the cool night. Ruth had given her a skein of beautiful orange, red, and yellow yarn and a hook. Then, she'd patiently taught Charlotte how to count the stitches in each row so the scarf had straight edges. It had taken Charlotte hours longer than she would have guessed. Finishing the project had made her feel accomplished in a way she hadn't since arriving in Minden. Even before the note, it served as another reminder that she couldn't stay in this charming town forever. She *needed* to be achieving; she felt aimless without goals to chase.

The street was filled with the evidence that summer had officially given way to fall. To most, Main Street in Minden was nothing more than a street sign displayed below the blinking orange traffic light at the intersection with the highway. To the residents of Minden, the thriving Main Street served as a reminder that their little town could survive. Even when so many others had faded away with only abandoned storefronts and empty lots as testimony to the communities once centered there. Small businesses still lined the road and the residents of Minden and the surrounding area were fiercely loyal to their local shops.

Shop windows filled with straw bales, fake spider webs, and scarecrows complemented the crunch of dry leaves on their stroll. Luke deliberately stepped in piles of leaves gathered against the brick and stone buildings. He pulled Charlotte off course to step in a particular promising bunch of leaves. Charlotte rolled her eyes at the boyish habit, but Luke gave her a grin and encouraged her to give in to the frivolity. Her stylish gray, heeled boots didn't have quite the same impact as his heavy work boots, but it made her smile regardless. After their walk, Luke drove her back to the cottage and kissed her goodnight. His lips were warm and soft, inviting her to linger in his embrace. It was over too soon, and Luke drove away; leaving her once more to thoughts she couldn't avoid.

Charlotte sat perched on the sofa in the dark and

stared at the opened letter, still sitting on the coffee table where she had dropped it hours ago. She turned options over and over in her head. *I could ignore it. No one knows I got the letter. Or I could go back. I could confront Anna, now. Right?* The thought of redemption was enticing. Could she confront Anna? *Who am I kidding, I can't show my face there. They all think I betrayed the company. But I didn't. I didn't do anything. This isn't my fault. I hate her. I hate her. I hate her!* Immediately, she flinched at that thought. It was so ugly, so much different and darker than any thoughts she'd had since her lunch with Luke.

Her time in Minden had dulled the edge of her hurt and anger, but it cut sharply now, honed by the not-so-gentle reminder that the world—her world—moved on without her. Charlotte paced the cottage and eventually found herself on the porch, fuming in the silence until it grew stifling. Exhausted, she finally collapsed into bed and promised to decide tomorrow.

The next morning, Charlotte was determined to suppress her problem again. She accompanied Ruth to church and sat next to Luke. His warm voice gliding over the words of each worship song made her stomach flutter. The first time she'd gone to church, she'd listened to the songs, not really knowing what most of the words meant. Today, she heard familiar words from verses she'd read over the last few weeks. One song had played on the radio in Luke's car on their way to dinner last night. Charlotte quietly sang the refrain "You are my everything and I will adore You" and let those words pour over her worried spirit and quiet the restless thoughts about the future and the lawsuit. *You are my everything.* Was that true? Could that be enough? Maybe, if God was her everything, Charlotte didn't need to go back. All she needed was to be right here, in this warm and welcoming church, next to Luke and worshiping the God she'd recently encountered.

But, when the glow of Sunday morning wore off, Charlotte's thoughts circled back to the lawsuit and her failed career. Leaving that torn, frayed end of her time at Millennium ate at her. Luke tried to convince her over and over again that her ability to read people was a gift. She was starting to agree – the more she read, the more she reflected on her life and the realization that God made her, exactly as she was. With the ability to read people and the desire to achieve. That was the key. She still wanted to achieve something. And here in Minden? She wasn't achieving anything.

The thought of leaving Luke was too painful to think about for long, so Charlotte just didn't. Think about it, that is. As she packed her bags, she didn't think about it. As she loaded her car, she didn't think about it. Even as she left the key to the cottage on the counter, she didn't think about how much it would hurt Luke to find out she left. *My life is in St. Louis, God. I can't stay here! Even though I am happy here. I know Luke won't be with me, but You will, right? You have to be with me, I don't have anyone else.* Charlotte quickly wrote a note to Ruth, and one to Luke, leaving them beneath the key on the counter. Neither said all of the things she wanted them to, but at least they'd know she didn't leave without a thought to them. Then, with her new Bible in the passenger seat, Charlotte drove away from the cottage with tears in her eyes.

WHEN SHE DROVE across the bridge from Illinois, Charlotte passed the famous Arch. During her travels, the Arch always signified she was home and as much as it no longer felt like home; Charlotte smiled. It was familiar, at least. Her apartment was just as she'd left it, although her few houseplants had been left without a thought and were beyond hope at this point. The stark contrast between her St. Louis condo and her cottage in Minden was a bit unsettling. Her condo was filled with clean lines, modern furniture, and hardly a personal touch. Charlotte remembered the cozy feeling of the condo with the farmhouse table, soft linens, and warm colors with longing. *I'll just redecorate this place to fit my new style. I can make this place homier, surely. Eventually.* Right now, she needed to get to work.

Charlotte pulled her laptop out of her bag and set it up in its former place at her desk. She skimmed emails on her personal account, none too important, and a couple where people reached out about the impending lawsuit. Charlotte began to formulate a plan, and resisted the urge to immediately call Millennium and leave a message for her former boss – the CEO. The last time they talked, her mentor and friend had looked at her with pity, as though she were a wounded puppy. Charlotte had let a few tears escape before calling the meeting short and leaving. *For a strong, career woman – is there anything more humiliating than crying at work?* She wondered how Roger would regard her if and when they were together again. Disdain? Anger? The pity was probably gone by now, since she was now (as far as he knew) to blame for their legal troubles. Now, she had to figure out how to explain everything, and hopefully make things right. Charlotte knew she might not be to blame for the situation – no, that honor belongs solely to Anna, but it was surely her responsibility to fix it. She didn't know when she'd be able to make that call, but before she could; she had to unravel the mess that was her last six months at Millennium.

18

———————

The next week and a half felt like six months to Luke. A thousand times, he quickly tapped out a message on his phone to Charlotte before deleting it slowly, one letter at a time. They were all various drafts of the same message. *Where are you? Come back, please. You aren't ready to be on your own.*

If you were to ask him, the letter Charlotte left was crap. A few platitudes about having to go back to "real life" and fix things she broke. Charlotte needed to achieve something, to accomplish something in the face of difficult challenges. Okay, maybe that wasn't crap. Luke couldn't imagine Charlotte not doing amazing things. She was too smart; too hard-working. Charlotte also wrote some words about being grateful for their 'friendship' and for teaching her about her Savior. Luke smiled, remembering their lunch and following afternoon when Charlotte had opened her heart. As he replayed the scenes from the day, he got to the kiss in the garden and absently rubbed his chest as though he could massage away the ache. *Father, why did you bring her here and make me fall in love with her if you were just going to take her away again?* He closed his eyes. *Wait. Fall in love? Am I in love with Charlotte? Oh God, I am. But she's not here. Why did you do this? Tell me what I am supposed to do.*

Luke waited in silence, begging for an answer. A minute passed. Then two. He stretched, feeling the familiar strain of tired muscles. He had worked all day, all week actually, hoping the manual labor would drive away the incessant thoughts of Charlotte. Of her in the cabin. Of kissing her in the garden. Of her sliming him with pumpkin goo. Of glancing at her during the prayer at the softball game to see her blush. *God, please! You took Rachel away from me, you can't take Charlotte too. I was broken after Rachel died. I needed her too much. I don't need Charlotte like that, though. I'm much more mature in my faith now, Father.* And then it hit him in waves. Luke was more mature now. He didn't rely on her for his relationship with Christ like he had once relied on Rachel. *But she isn't, is she? Oh God, I haven't been praying for her this week. Only myself. I'm so incredibly selfish – please forgive me! Father, show me how to pray for her. What does she need?* Luke answered his own question. *She needs You. Be close to her, help her feel Your presence. Remind Charlotte of the grace You give, of the relationship she has with You. Help her find a church. It's Saturday night... I wonder if she even realizes it.* As Luke continued to pray, he knew what to do. He quickly looked up the reference of the verse he was thinking of and typed it out. Looking at the message waiting only for him to hit send; it felt too impersonal. He moved his cursor back to the beginning and added another verse; one he knew by heart because Ruth wrote it in every Christmas, birthday, and anniversary card she ever sent him.

IT DIDN'T TAKE LONG for Charlotte to get back into the groove. Yoga in the morning, shower, work, have dinner delivered by a nearby restaurant and eat it in front of the computer as she read the news of the day before collapsing into her chic, modern platform bed.

It was Saturday night before Charlotte even stopped to think. A simple text from Luke interrupted her lo mein and MSNBC. It was the carbon copy of a thousand lonely nights before Minden.

Phil 1:3

Hebrews 10:24-25

Charlotte's heart sank and she slithered from the couch to the floor, staring blankly at her phone. Even though she had no idea what those verses said; the mere presence of a text from Luke with the now familiar code of chapter and verse made her both want to smile and weep. *I haven't thought of Luke all week...* She was thinking of him now. Missing his smile and his laugh. Even his surly stubborness. *But, I haven't thought of God either. I'm such a failure. Why did I think I could be Christian and still be ME? The me, that is, who kicks butt and take names in the boardroom?* Charlotte wanted to be both. She wanted to be successful and important. *Maybe it's impossible. Maybe that is why I never see Christians in my previous world... They all have to live in the middle of nowhere with jobs that aren't stressful and where Sunday is a day off, instead of a day to catch up because the phones are quiet in the office.* But that didn't seem right either. Charlotte thought of Joe. He'd been successful. A leader. He'd lived in this world and kept his faith strong. What was she missing?

Charlotte walked into the bedroom and grabbed her Bible, from where it laid buried in the still mostly unpacked suitcase. She looked again at the verses Luke had sent her.

She finally found the small book and her finger found Philippians 1:3. She read it out loud to the empty space. "I thank my God every time I remember you."

Charlotte grinned. *Leave it to Luke to find a Bible verse that is actually a personal message.* Moving on to the next verse, she found Hebrews 10:24-25. "And let us consider how we may spur one another on toward love and good deeds – not giving up meeting as some are in the habit of doing, but encouraging one another – and all the more as you see the Day approaching."

What did Luke want me to get out of this verse? Is he just asking how he can encourage me? Charlotte read it again and was caught by the interjection in the middle. *Not giving up meeting as some are in the habit of doing.* Like he was standing there with a neon sign, Charlotte realized why Luke had texted her. She searched "church near me" and was quickly overwhelmed by the results. Baptist, Methodist,

Presbyterian. The church they'd attended in Minden had been the Baptist church, so she selected one nearby and made note of the service time.

Charlotte continued flipping through her precious purple Bible, enjoying the passages highlighted and the notes scrawled in margins. When she was almost done and getting ready to wrap it up for the night, Charlotte's noticed a few pages stuck together in the front. She carefully separated the thin pages and began to read.

THIS BIBLE BELONGS to
   Rachel Marie Coffman
   Presented as a gift on
   April 16th, 2001
   On the occasion of
   Her baptism
   By
   Her loving parents

SHE STARED AT THE NAME, written in delicate blue ink. Ruth and Luke had given her Rachel's Bible? The note written below the completed form made her cry at the gift this beautiful woman had given her, despite having never met.

RACHEL,

We are so proud of the young woman you have become. Follow Him, and he will make your paths straight. Know that we are always here for you, and we love you unconditionally.

Mom and Dad

CHARLOTTE THOUGHT back to when they had given her the Bible. Luke had to have known that it was Rachel's Bible being handed over. But he hadn't cared. It had been hard for Charlotte to believe he could really let go of Rachel and be happy with her. This was a big, bold affirmative in that sense. There had been no jealousy, no trace of sorrow in his expression as Ruth handed the Bible to Charlotte. Not that it mattered now. Che was here in the city, and she wasn't going back to Minden. She wasn't a small-town girl. Charlotte needed to chase her goals and use the gifts God had given her. And that meant taking back her career.

THE NEXT MORNING, Charlotte arrived at the Washington Summit Baptist Church a few minutes before 9:30. The first thing she noticed was that the church felt similar to Minden Baptist. There were pews and hymnals in the seats. But, it was definitely different too. For one thing, there was a choir in long robes settling in to an area at the front of the church. Looking around at the crowd of unfamiliar faces, Charlotte debated leaving; but when the music started, she couldn't bring herself to. *This ought to be interesting,* she thought as she slid into a pew in the back row.

Quickly, Charlotte forgot that she was an outsider and that she didn't know the songs they were singing. She simply closed her eyes and listened. She listened to the choir and the strong solid voice of the woman to her right. Old women shouted "Amen" and "Sing it", and then marveled at the constant, quiet whisper of dozens of people murmuring "Thank you, Jesus. Yes, Father, we need you" during the prayer. While the preacher spoke, she had to contain her laughter the first time someone shouted at him a hearty "Preach it!" and then a similar "Mmmmhmm, I heard that."

The marvel of it, to Charlotte, wasn't in the words the preacher spoke or in the beauty of the music. But, she was once again reminded that she wasn't alone in her faith. While she had no idea what these people did for a living, she at least knew they lived in the city. It was enough for now.

After the service ended, Charlotte was waiting to exit her pew when someone said her name. "Charlotte?" She looked up and recognized Janise, who worked in IT at Millennium. They'd been friendly, although not especially close. "What are you doing here?" Charlotte read her expression quickly and then, seeing only curiosity without animosity in her eyes, responded.

"Just visiting. I wanted to go to church this morning, and this is pretty close to my condo." She hesitated, then continued. "Plus I, uh, went to a Baptist church pretty often while I was on leave." *And I didn't think I would have missed it this much.*

"Well, I for one am really glad you are back. I never believed what they said about you – you were loyal to Mr. Daniels to a fault, if I remember correctly. When do you come back to Millennium?" Janise asked the question as though Charlotte's return was a given. And Charlotte hadn't realized how much she had doubted it herself.

"Oh, wow. Thanks for saying that. I know it looks pretty bad. I've been trying to work out how to prove my innocence, but it's been hard with only my files and memory to work from. I'm not sure if I'll be able to actually come back, but I have to try to fix this." Charlotte's voice trembled, revealing how much she cared.

Janise listened and her brown eyes softened at Charlotte's tone. "You want to grab lunch with me? I'd love to hear what really happened." Charlotte looked at Janise again, and instead of the microexpressions and physical signals she typically saw without thinking—Charlotte saw only a friend.

GOD MUST HAVE SENT Charlotte an angel in the form of Janise. After explaining the whole story to her over salads (and a shared side of French fries), Janise had offered up her IT expertise and access to look into Charlotte's claims. It was very different from the lunch dates Charlotte remembered with Anna.

Charlotte met Anna on their first day at Millennium. They made small talk over the HR paperwork and talked about how excited they were about the chance to work there. They went out for drinks after work that day. Charlotte had never felt so at ease with anyone but her sisters. They laughed and joked like old friends, making fun of the names of ridiculous drinks at the happy-hour bar they'd found around the corner. "What the heck even is a 'Salty Dog'? Sounds like a bad food cart!" Anna joked.

Charlotte skimmed the list of drinks and put on her best prim and proper fake British accent, "Yes, good sir. I'd like one 'Juicy Lucy'." They both broke down in giggles. At twenty-two, coming from their first day of a real 'grown-up' job, they were on top of the world and nothing could bring them down.

Anna mentioned needing to find an apartment nearby and Charlotte eagerly shared that she was looking too and wouldn't it be great if they just got a place together to save money? Years later, they each bought their own places, but not before the friendship was set in stone. Charlotte recalled frivolous shopping trips to Chicago, many nights hitting the clubs in St. Louis, and long days grinding out reports together for Millennium. Looking back, though, Charlotte couldn't remember very many deep conversations. She'd never felt comfortable telling Anna about her family. Anna was a presence, and Charlotte's natural insecurity made her feel lucky just to tag along for the ride most of the time. Anna would find a boyfriend for a few months and Charlotte wouldn't see her much. But when Anna came over with a broken heart and a renewed vow to stay away from men forever, Charlotte would dig out the ice cream and commiserate with her friend, enjoying the time they spent together before Anna was involved in another whirlwind romance.

Lunch with Janise was comfortable, and felt more genuine despite the brevity of their budding friendship. Janise confessed the struggles she was having with her boss, who seemed determined to make her miserable, and Charlotte told her about Minden and Luke. She told Janise that she'd only recently become a Christian and was finding it hard to feel her faith now that she was back in St. Louis.

Janise nodded in understanding. "It's really hard, that's for sure. But I think that it's hard no matter where you are. You've been hiding away somewhere with no job, no responsibilities. That's not real life, woman! And everyone has to figure out what it means to follow God and still live their life. Even stay-at-home moms struggle with it. Keep reading and praying and you'll do just find. Plus, the sooner we get this resolved, the sooner you can figure out your new normal." Charlotte held eagerly to Janise's reassurances. "I'm not making any promises, but we should have information on the server that can help. The truth shall set you free, Charlie." Janise giggled at her own profound statement, and Charlotte smiled. How amazing it felt to have an ally!

The next weekend, Charlotte returned to the same church and sat with Janise. A Deacon in the church announced that the sermon today would be a different pastor than last week. Then, the Deacon gave an update on the on-going search for a new pastor. He explained that the firm they had hired to conduct the search was currently screening candidates and that the first round of interviews would start next week. Charlotte had never considered exactly how churches found their pastors, but before she could dwell on it for long, the teaching started and she found herself engrossed in what the guest speaker was saying. But she tucked the information away for the future.

19

After church Charlotte returned to her condo and grabbed lunch. Just as she began to dive in to the paperwork again, her phone rang. Her face broke into a broad smile when she saw the caller ID.

She greeted him first. "Hello, Joe! It is good to hear from you. I've actually been meaning to call you!" Charlotte let her smile fill her voice.

Joe exhaled a laugh. "You have? About what?"

"Believe it or not, I became a Christian!"

Now, it was Joe's voice that was filled with joy. "That's great news, Charlotte." Then, he admitted, "I've been praying for you every day."

Charlotte was stunned. She was so used to people being selfish and uncaring. "Wow, that's really amazing. Thank you!" Then, she realized he had called her, and curiosity niggled at her. "Are you calling for anything in particular?"

Joe laughed, "Actually, I just had the feeling I needed to catch up with you again. I guess I know why! What are you doing these days?"

"Well, I'm back in St. Louis and trying to fix this mess I left behind at Millennium." She tried not to let her current discouraged mood leak into the conversation.

"Ahh, yes – the lawsuit. What happened with all that, anyway?"

Charlotte explained what she knew so far, that a coworker had quietly undermined her performance and leaked the document, though she didn't yet have proof.

Joe let out a low whistle. "Wow. That's quite a story. Do you think Roger will believe you?"

Charlotte bit her cheek. "I don't know. I want to say yes, but then, I've been wrong before. It's the truth, though."

"I know." He thought for a minute and then asked, "Will you stay with Millennium?"

That question had been turning around in her mind as often as the question about how Anna had managed to get the document. "I'm not sure. In some ways, Millennium doesn't feel like the place for me anymore." She considered it. "If not Millennium, then where? I want to use my experience and abilities, you know?" Then, an idea flashed in her thoughts. "You know, I learned something today about how big churches find pastors – they use recruiting firms just like companies do."

Joe gave a non-committal sound. "Actually, I did know that. In fact, I might have someone you should talk to." He went on to explain that he had been an elder for his large church during an executive pastor search.

They wrapped up their conversation and Charlotte thanked him profusely. Everything was falling into place and her excitement for the future grew.

Charlotte returned to the files with renewed fervor. She worked backwards, starting with the case that ended it all; trying to figure out how the document had been leaked. She remembered her ally and friend and texted her for help. Janise pulled the server log from Charlotte's protected drive. Janise's name showed up on her caller ID shortly after.

"It looks bad, Charlotte. It was your profile that was logged into the server, and the file was copied to a flashdrive from your laptop name and IP address at the office. Hard to say it wasn't you based on that information..." Janise didn't sound upset, or even suspicious. "Whoever did this sure covered their tracks well. Can you think of anyone that would have access to your login information? I don't know how Anna could have done this. Sure, she's smart - but I never got the feeling she was real good with computers. Unfortunately, I can't access any of your email or calendar files anymore. The company still has them, but they were migrated to our off-site server for long term storage. I'm sure they will get subpoenaed in the lawsuit though..."

Charlotte's heart sank at the news. She should have expected nothing less from Anna - she was detail oriented, that was for sure. Charlotte had been positive the computer log would exonerate her. Of course, Roger would have checked that before throwing her out, right?

Janise continued, "I'll keep trying to find something on my end, okay? Don't give up."

Charlotte wasn't going to do that, but she was discouraged at the news from Janise. "I won't. But I'll talk to you later, okay?"

If Janise can't find anything in the computers to prove my innocence, I guess it is up to me. For the next week, Charlotte poured over documents, racking her brain for clues as to how to show that

Anna had been sabotaging her. Charlotte tackled the stacks of files that still remained in her condo office. When she came across a discrepancy, she highlighted it. Once she found the pattern, it wasn't nearly as hard as she had expected. Charlotte was double checking the work history on a candidate for a Sales Manager position when the sharp rap on the door startled her from her intense focus. She opened the door without looking through the peephole, a habit she must have lost during her months in Minden. Seeing who waited on the other side, Charlotte attempted to undo her mistake. Anna wedged her stiletto heel in the door, preventing it from closing. Charlotte sighed and then opened the door further. "What are you doing here, Anna?"

"I should ask you the same thing, Charlie." Her name was said with a sneer, the use of it over her formal name a painful reminder of the relationship she had once shared with this woman. All pretense of innocence was gone since the last time Charlotte had seen Anna in her office before leaving.

"It's my house." Charlotte wasn't giving an inch. She wasn't angry, just determined. God had been working on her anger over the last few weeks and she was surprised at the lack of reaction seeing Anna was causing.

"I heard you were back, and I just want to remind you—you are done. Don't think just because Roger didn't fire you that you can come back. You are the reason Millennium is in this mess and no one—especially Roger—wants to see you come back. So just forget it."

"Gee, thanks for the tip. You're a real pal." Sarcasm was a sharp tool Charlotte rarely utilized, but it came out before she could bite it back.

"Why don't you climb back into whatever hole you were hiding in, and let the rest of us who are actually good at our jobs handle this?" Anna must have been satisfied with the hurt look on Charlotte's face and confident that she'd had the last word. With a smug smile, Anna walked out of Charlotte's condo. The words felt like a bowling ball to the gut and all the doubts that Charlotte harbored for months during her descent to rock bottom resurfaced in an instant.

But just as quickly, new thoughts took their place. Luke's reassurance that her abilities were a gift. Self-affirmations that she was just as talented and hard-working as she'd ever been. Charlotte's attitude and work ethic had taken her to the top once before and Anna wasn't going to drag her down again. Despite Anna's intentions of scaring Charlotte once and for all, she only succeeded at motivating Charlotte more. Charlotte knew she was good at her job and now the truth was going to come out. It was only a matter of time before Anna had to admit it, too.

Charlotte returned to her paperwork. After a few more days of double-checking work and piecing together a timeline of the lies, she felt like she had a pretty solid case against Anna. She texted Janise.

Good news. I think I have enough to prove Anna was the culprit, even with the IT logs contradicting me.

Janise didn't respond, but Charlotte put it out of her mind and called to schedule a meeting with Roger. There was still no proof that Charlotte hadn't leaked the document, but there was definitely proof that Anna was doctoring reports and negatively impacting the selection process.

20

Charlotte's cell phone rang at eight o'clock that night while she was rewarding her hard work with a sushi dinner at her favorite Japanese restaurant. She saw Millennium's number and answered warily, "This is Charlotte Walters."

Charlotte immediately heard the tremor in Janise's voice. "Charlotte, I'm so sorry."

"What do you mean, what's going on?"

"Anna wasn't working alone. I just couldn't figure out how she had gotten access to your accounts so I kept digging. It turns out that Paul—my boss—was in on the whole thing. I used our security software and found the text messages on their company phones."

"This is crazy, Janise. Why would Paul be

working with Anna? I wouldn't even think she would know who he was." Paul was definitely not Anna's type. Anna went for flashy, successful business-types who played golf on the weekends and showered her with expensive gifts. Paul was quiet and dorky. From what Charlotte remembered, he spent his weekends playing board games and watching movies.

"As far as I can tell, she was using him. He thought their relationship was real." Janise admitted, "I feel kind of bad for the guy. I mean, he must have been stressed out about what he did, and Anna ghosted him right after you let. I think that's why he's been a nightmare to work for since then. Paul found me digging through the access records and freaked out." Janise's voice elevated. "He threatened to fire me! But look, Paul reset your passwords and gave Anna access to your files that day. Then, he reset it again and you had to create a new password when you logged back in that afternoon! " Janise was sobbing at this point and the rest of her story came out in spurts. "He took my phone. He saw your text message and called her. Anna knows you have proof." She tried to compose herself. "I don't know what they're going to do. You've got to stop them. They just left the office. I'm so sorry, Charlotte."

Charlotte threw some cash down on the table

and abandoned her sashimi platter and ran out of the restaurant. She ran as fast as she could in her heels to make it the five blocks back to her condo. Briefly, she registered the broken door frame before she cautiously stepped into the small entry way. The condo was still dark and her winded breaths sounded impossibly loud in the silent space. Slipping off her heels, Charlotte crept into the open-concept living room. She heard a man's voice coming from the office, to her left.

"I don't know what I'm looking for, Anna. All I see is a bunch of papers and a laptop." The voice paused, and then continued. "Of course I love you, baby. Please don't cry. I'll just get everything I can carry and you can figure out if it's important, okay? I'll meet you in an hour." Another pause. "I'll hurry. She was gone when I got here, but I'm not sure when she'll be back."

Charlotte listened silently at the door and pulled out her cell phone as she backed into the bathroom just down the hallway. After whispering her address and that there was an intruder to the 911 operator, she returned to the office and decided to confront Paul. *God, I sure hope this is the right move. Please keep me safe.*

"The police are on their way." Thankfully, her voice sounded a lot more confident than she felt.

Paul whirled at the sound with wide eyes.

"You don't have to do this, you know." Charlotte kept her gaze on his, but noticed with relief that he didn't have a weapon of any sort. She read his expressions. Panic, fear, guilt.

"Yes, I do. Anna will never forgive me if I don't go through with it. She said this is the last obstacle to us being together for good. That she was only ignoring me because there were loose ends."

"Okay, okay. I can see that you love her very much." Paul nodded.

"I'd do anything for her." She saw the truth of that statement in his eyes.

"That's very romantic. Would she do the same for you?" Charlotte watched the doubt cloud his expression. "Where is she, anyway? Weren't you together at the office just a bit ago?"

"She had to go feed her cat."

Charlotte nearly laughed. "Anna's allergic to cats, Paul. She lied to you. Anna just didn't want to be the one caught breaking and entering."

Paul shook his head. "No. She had to feed her cat!" He spoke with absolute conviction

"Okay, okay." Charlotte tried to change her approach. "Paul, the police will be here any second. You can go to prison, or you can leave now and I won't say anything about your involvement in this." She watched the indecision war in his eyes as he glanced to the door behind her. Charlotte stepped to the side. "Anna won't wait for you if you go to jail." Charlotte tried desperately to get through to him. "Paul, she doesn't love you. She's just using you - like she used me all those years. Don't you see? You deserve someone so much better." Charlotte pulled every bit of information she remembered about Paul from her mental file on him. "Someone who appreciates your sense of humor and gets your jokes about Star Wars." She took a stab in the dark. "Have you seen her at all since I left? Or did she only come back once she knew I was in town again trying to prove my innocence?"

Paul's jaw tightened before he exhaled and seemed to deflate before her. His bravado was gone and she saw the familiar IT supervisor she remembered from before. "I'll go." Charlotte stepped aside and let him pass. "For what it's worth - I'm sorry. I never had anything against you."

Charlotte laid a hand on his shoulder. "I know. It's okay. I forgive you. Just go, before the police get here." He went back out the front door and down the steps.

Sirens wailed in the distance, getting louder as they approached her building. She opened the window to the fire escape and then stood in the hallway outside her busted door and greeted the police as they came up the stairs. She let them do a sweep of her apartment looking for the long-gone intruder and then went in to confirm that nothing was missing. Since nothing was taken, the police warned her that there was not much they could do. Her building didn't have any security cameras. They assumed the intruder had heard her call 911 and then exited the window before they had a chance to take anything. Charlotte didn't say anything to correct their assumption.

CHARLOTTE GOT a text the next morning from Janise's email account.

I found something last night. Can you come to the office before your meeting?

Curious what Janise could have found, Charlotte got to the office early. Since she didn't work there anymore, she was given a visitor badge by the front desk and asked to sign in. The cold treatment stung as she took in the familiar surroundings. These were her stomping grounds. Or at least they used to be. *Father, I am going to need You today. Help me know what to say. Help me be patient and not be quick to anger. Help Roger see that I am right and that Anna is to blame!* She knew her prayer was petty and self-serving, but she didn't know what else to pray at this point. Hopefully God understood. As she waited, Charlotte mentally rehearsed all the things she planned to say. In her rehearsal, she appeared calm, collected, professional – and right. And in her mind, Roger sat there and listened and nodded along in agreement as she explained.

Janise came to the waiting room and found her. "Here, I managed to get this printed before Paul found me last night. It's the log of the file breach and the password resets. I thought it might help. Plus, I found a box of your office stuff in storage. Can you think of anything from your office that might help?"

Charlotte studied the log and her heart sank. "It still says that charlotte.walters accessed the file on August 2nd."

"...Any chance you weren't in the office on August 2nd?" Janise joked.

Charlotte jumped, pulled from her thoughts at the last question. "I don't know, but I can find out where I was!" Quickly giving Janise instructions of what to look for, she sat back down, thankful she still had fifteen minutes before her meeting. Hopefully that would give Janise enough time to find what she needed and get back before the meeting started. She paced for a moment, but then Charlotte sat back down just before Roger's assistant came to take her back to the conference room, with Janise no where in sight.

21

Charlotte was led into the conference room and Roger was there, along with an angry-looking Anna. *I can't believe she came. I wonder if Paul talked to her. Actually... maybe this is better.* Charlotte smiled genuinely and greeted Roger.

"Roger, thank you for seeing me. I know what you must think, but I'm here to explain – like I should have done months ago."

"I'm not sure an explanation can change anything, but you've done too much for this firm for me to not hear you out." Roger said almost reluctantly.

Charlotte pulled her laptop out of her bag and began to hook it up.

"What are you doing?" Anna accused. "You

don't have permission to give a presentation or whatever this is."

Charlotte just looked at Roger, who nodded. "It's fine. I want to hear her out."

When the computer was set up, Charlotte began. "I should have done this in the beginning, when things first went haywire – but I was too afraid. I was mortified that I had let this happen. My reputation was shattered and I didn't know how to recover. But I don't care if it is hard, and I don't care if I have to fight tooth and nail to take back what I worked for." She already knew she would do whatever it took.

"What I'm going to show you today is the whole story. Not just the pieces you already know, but everything that happened and then, I'm going to help Millennium fix it." The fervor in her voice was unmistakable.

"It started almost 18 months ago. I was working on the Executive Sales Director position for Parthenon, do you remember?" she waited for a nod from Roger and then continued. On the screen, Charlotte pulled up a copy of the research document on Bill Baird; the eventual candidate selected for the position. "Here you can see the notes on Bill from research. In these notes, it hints that Bill has an alcohol problem. He doesn't. It attributes the failing of his first company to his mismanagement—when anyone in the industry will tell you it was the unfortunate timing of a tornado." Charlotte waited for Roger to absorb the report. "Honestly, I never read this—because I knew Bill from a previous search and had already mentally advanced him to the next phase." And then, she dropped the hammer. "Anna completed these reports and filled them with lies about the most qualified candidates. I remember the second stage of the process it was extremely obvious that Bill was the front-runner. Would he have been if I had seen the true information about the other candidates? I'm not sure." Charlotte pulled a printed set of documents from her bag, as Anna began to protest.

"This is ridiculous, this is all subject to interpretation. So I made a mistake on Bill's report; that doesn't mean anything!"

Charlotte continued as though Anna hadn't spoken. "Here is a copy of all of the research from that project, with the lies I identified highlighted. As a side note: some of those are extremely qualified candidates, and you should definitely consider them for future positions." She pulled more documents from her bag.

"Here are the files from the Technical Officer at ReGlow; the Human Resources Officer at KBH, and the CFO for Kintern." For emphasis, Charlotte dropped them out on the table one at a time, each hitting with a satisfying smack. Each file was at least a half inch thick. "Each of them with significant falsehoods making the strongest candidates look weak, and some making weak candidates look better."

Anna tried to speak but was silenced by a glare from Roger. Roger flipped through the documents. "How does this turn into the situation with Byte?"

"Great question. By this time, I've made Anna my right-hand on any big cases. I never suspected anything." Charlotte pulled even more documents out of her bag. "I let Anna conduct second-stage interviews, and I took her feedback as accurate. We had interviewed together enough times over ten years that I trusted her insight; and these weren't the final interviews. Slowly, my success rate dropped as I placed candidates in positions they weren't prepared for. And then, I was given the Development Officer position at Byte. I had to nail it. So, I convinced them to give me the classified development plan for the next ten years – so I could really find the person with the skillset that matched their future. I needed this placement, more than any one before, to be successful long-term." Charlotte turned her gaze to Roger. Silently pleading with him to believe her. "I would never betray the reputation of this firm, and I don't know exactly how Anna got access to the document. I completed every step of that project myself. I did the initial research and I conducted all interviews and evaluations myself. But the same day I recommended Nick Moser as the CDO; the development plan was leaked."

At that moment, Janise knocked on the door and held up a notebook for Charlotte to see. Charlotte waved her in.

"What's all this, Charlotte? Who is this?" Roger asked.

"This is Janise, she works in IT here." Janise gave an embarrassed wave and went to stand in the corner, as though scared of the table.

"Here are the IT logs that show when the file was copied from my laptop here at the office, using my login."

Charlotte spotted Anna's smug smile. With a smirk of her own, Charlotte handed the paper access log to Roger and grabbed the notebook from where Janise had set it on the table. Roger had tried to convince her more than once that she was living in the dark ages using a paper calendar. Since the day she started working, she had kept a daily planner in addition to her electronic appointment system in her email, often taking a fair bit of teasing for it. But now, she prayed it would have some of the answers she needed.

She flipped the cover open, remembering how she had loved choosing her new planner in December every year. It was her gift to herself each Christmas. As a little girl, she loved new school supplies. The fresh start – a box of unbroken, perfectly sharpened crayons, which then migrated to clean, untarnished notebooks waiting to be filled with class notes. Always starting in precise, neat handwriting that devolved into frantic, lazier scribbles as the semester wore on. Over the years, her planner had operated in much the same way; except that each year her ability to remain neat and organized and methodical within the planner became better and better. Her most recent entries were just as neat as the first ones in January. She flipped to the month of August. Charlotte laid her eyes on the date in question.

8:30 *Final interview – Nick Moser – Conference Room 3*

Noon – Lunch with Anna (Byte CDO decision)

1:00 *Leadership Strategy Meeting with Roger – R's Office*

She remembered that lunch. Having decided that before making the decision, she wanted to talk through the entire thing with Anna. They left after her final interview with Nick and went to a small café near the office that served wonderful salads and wraps. At the time, Charlotte thought that Anna had been a perfect listener, not saying much but letting Charlotte work through the decision-making process as a supportive confidant. In retrospect, Charlotte wondered what she'd missed. Had there been guilt in her eyes, or even hatred?

Since Roger held the IT log, she asked him, "Roger, what time was the file copied?"

He skimmed the document. "10:42 AM on August 2nd."

Charlotte looked at the appointment calendar again and then silently thanked God. "The computer copy of my calendar can confirm, as can the current CDO of Byte technology, that while the file was being copied, I was firmly ensconced in the final interview with Nick Moser."

Anna broke her silence, "A lot of times you have your laptop in interviews. That doesn't prove anything."

Charlotte nodded. "That's true. I do sometimes have my laptop during interviews. But I never have my laptop during final interviews. And even if I did have it with me, there is no way I could have accessed the network and copied the file. Do you know why, Roger?" She held the planner across the table, open to August 2nd.

Roger looked at the planner and saw the same vindicating evidence that Charlotte had. "There is no network access from conference room 3," Roger whispered the thought, something that had always irked him and he complained about often. "The basement walls are too thick to get a signal. Charlotte, why on earth did you hold your interview in that conference room?"

"I was so tired of making the wrong decisions on recent accounts that I didn't want to leave anything to chance. I picked the conference room with as few distractions as possible – no traffic outside the door that might catch his eye or mine. No cell phones ringing. Just me, and Nick having a conversation about the future of Byte Technology in the basement." Charlotte smiled. "And it worked. Nick is the perfect CDO, with or without a leaked development plan. He can attest that he and I were in that conference room, without interruption from 8:30 until nearly noon.

"Roger, I know it is hard to believe, but this was a long-term, strategic plan to undermine your confidence in MY ability. And I let it happen, but that doesn't mean you have to pay the price. It started with the candidate profiles being altered to hurt my decision making, and since I locked up the Byte interviews and handled absolutely everything myself, Anna had to find another way to interfere."

Roger looked at Anna once more, not saying anything – but letting the silence and the set of his jaw request a response.

Anna was practically vibrating, and Charlotte could see the tell-tale indicator of someone biting back words. And she could see when Anna lost control and gave into the impulse to speak up. Charlotte flinched at the unrestrained venom in the eyes of her former best friend.

"Why did you have to come back!? It was perfect. Without perfect little 'Miss. I-see-everything", I finally had the chance to be Roger's right hand. To get the big placements!" Anna stood, her voice rising. She had always been calm and collected. Never out of control at work that Charlotte could remember. "All I ever wanted was to not be in Charlotte's shadow, Roger!" Roger's eyes were wide, watching the scene unfold before him. His mouth hung open. Charlotte realized he would have never seen this side of Anna before. "I would do anything for this company. I didn't know they would sue us for the development plan! I just figured we would lose the account and that Charlotte would get fired once and for all." Anna was yelling now, and practically in tears. Then, she quieted. "I'm so sorry, Roger. Don't hate me! Please, just give me a chance to—"

Roger lifted a hand from where it was rubbing his temples, taking command of the room as he was apt to do. "Stop. Anna, just stop. You have one hour to clear out your office. Security will meet you there to supervise. You need to leave. We will deal with the lawsuit and your responsibility later." He calmly picked up the conference room phone and called security. Since Anna was still sobbing and pleading, he altered his instructions to have security meet Anna in the conference room and escort her instead.

Charlotte waited while all of this happened, and she felt justified and then shortly after – pity. *Why do I feel sorry for her? She did this to me! I shouldn't have to feel sorry for her. And yet, I do.* Charlotte spoke quietly, not looking at Anna while she continued to beg for understanding. "Anna?" She waited for Anna to quiet, then looked at her with a tilted head. She reached her hand out on the table, toward the woman she once called a friend. "You know, I really thought we were friends. I really thought I was lucky to be able to work with you and teach you what I knew. I'm so sorry you felt you had no option but to knock me down in order to rise yourself."

Anna's sobs subsided and the cold, manipulative woman re-emerged. Anna scoffed. "You're sorry? You come here three months after the fact and you take everything away from me? This isn't over, Charlie. Not by a long shot."

22

Janise stepped out of her corner of the room at that point and tried to sneak out the door.

Roger spoke up. "Thanks for all your hard work. What's your name again?"

"Umm.. I'm Janise Collins."

"Good work, Janise." Janise slipped out the door with a pointed look at Charlotte, which she interpreted as 'you better call me later.'

Roger leaned back in the conference room chair, a smile on his face. "It's good to have you back, Charlie. I've missed you, and I hated thinking that you had betrayed me like that."

"I know, Roger. One of things that hurt most of all was knowing that you thought it was possible I had." Charlotte pulled one last document from her briefcase and handed it to him. "I wasn't sure I was going to give this to you. But I think I have to." It hadn't missed her careful ear when she had said without a thought "you should consider them for future positions." Not we. You. Even subconsciously, she didn't consider herself a part of the Millennium team anymore.

Roger barely glanced at the single sheet of paper before looking back at Charlotte, his eyes wide with genuine surprise. "A resignation letter?"

Charlotte nodded. "You didn't fire me when you should have, and for that I am grateful – truly. But I need to leave. I can't work here knowing that you didn't trust me. And I have other things in mind for my future."

Roger sat up straight. "Charlotte, wait. I'm sorry I assumed the worst about you, but can you blame me with the evidence that was-" Charlotte cut him off.

"It's okay. I forgive you. But I still have to go. I hope this information helps you settle the suit with Byte. I'll call them if you need me to and explain everything. But, these last few months have taught me more about myself than I thought I wanted to know. As much as I learned from you in the years you've mentored me, the lessons I've been taught since leaving were a thousand times more important. I know my purpose now, Roger! And I intend to chase it." *To glorify God with my actions and point people to Jesus.* It had seemed so foreign to her when Luke had expressed his purpose in those terms. But now? She finally understood.

Roger nodded. Then he stood and hugged her. "I appreciate you coming back and setting the record straight."

"I had to. I couldn't stand the thought of you hating me."

Roger shook his head. "I never hated you, Charlie. You're like a daughter to me."

Charlotte smiled and hugged him again. "Stay in touch, Roger."

"Back at you, kid." The familiar nickname made the tear that had been threatening to spill over her eyelash finally drop. Roger had called her 'kid' when he first met her in the campus mentoring program, but had finally stopped several years previously when she became more a partner than an understudy in his company. Charlotte sniffed, grabbed her now-empty briefcase, turned on her heel and walked out the offices of her former home for the last time.

Charlotte called Janise from the parking garage not 10 minutes later.

"So, what are you going to do now?"

"I've got a couple of phone calls to make, and then I'm going home." *To Minden.* "I'll let you know when I get there, okay?" Janise knew that Charlotte didn't mean her condo a few blocks from the office, as Charlotte had regaled her with the stories of Luke and the tiny, entertaining town in Indiana where she had found peace in the midst of turmoil. *Maybe Janise can come visit me in Minden. Miss Ruth would love her.*

Janise agreed. "Call me anytime, girl. I'm just so glad it worked out. Drive safe."

LUKE WAS IN HIS OFFICE, running his hand through already tousled hair as he performed the dreaded task of entering quotes into his system. Then, he'd have to enter orders and invoice customers for work being completed today. He was days behind but still couldn't find the motivation to make sure he got paid for the backbreaking work his team was doing. Luke pressed his fingers to his eyes and then wiped his hands down his face for the hundredth time today.

Charlotte stood in the doorway, watching him in total silence. She leaned on the doorjamb, grateful it was open so she could observe him without his knowledge. She looked around the small office, smiling at the disorganized stacks of paper on the floor next to the desk, and the obvious touch of Ruth, or Rachel, in the decorations – a Bible verse hand painted on some weathered looking wood, curtains framing the window in a cheery, yet masculine pattern. She noticed the hunch of Luke's shoulders and the heavy sighs he released every ten seconds. His back was to her, and she could see the spreadsheet program open on the computer. She longed to see his eyes, but also afraid of what emotions she would see there. *Please let him forgive me, Father. I love him.*

With that simple prayer and reminder in her heart, she quietly knocked on the wall beside the door with her knuckle, never looking away from his position across the room. Startled, but grateful for the interruption; Luke finished typing the line item he was on while saying "yeah, what's up?" even as he turned around. The last word died as he spotted her. Both of them, completely still, stared at each other.

Charlotte tried desperately to read him, to see happiness or anger or something! But, he was as unreadable as ever.

And then, without a word, Luke got up and cross the small room to her in two steps. He grabbed her around the waist and pulled her to his body. One hand came up to the back of her head and he pressed it to his chest as he kissed her hair.

Relishing the closeness after her time of exile, Charlotte felt more than heard him mumbling, "You came back. Thank God, you came back. Charlotte, honey. You came back."

Luke held her like that for what seemed like hours and seconds all at once, and then he pushed her back to look in her eyes, even while keeping his arm around her waist. The absence of their contact hit her with the blast of cool air in place of his warmth. His hand moved from the back of her head around to caress he cheek. "Are you really back, sweetheart?"

"I'm back." Charlotte spoke timidly, even though her heart soared with every endearment he showered on her. "I couldn't stay there without you."

"I missed you so much. I wanted to call. I wanted to get in the car and drag you back here, kicking and screaming. I almost did, too – before I remembered I didn't have an address. Did you know your St. Louis condo is unlisted?" he smiled at the unspoken admission that fact may have been the only thing preventing his desired barbaric action.

Charlotte studied his sheepish grin and smiled in return. "I missed you, too. I couldn't believe how much I missed you." Finally, Luke guided her chin with his hand and kissed her softly.

"I'm so glad you are here, sweetheart. When do you have to go back?" Even though he dreaded the answer, he had to know how long it would be before he had to say goodbye to her again.

"What do you mean?"

"Are you here for the weekend? The cabin is still set up for you. I didn't change anything. You can stay there on the weekends and drive back to the city during the week. After I sell my business here, I can move to St. Louis with you so you don't have to drive so many miles." He stated this as though it were a foregone conclusion. *When we get married, I'll move there.* He didn't want to scare her away with those thoughts yet, but they were there. They'd been there since that night in the garden, surrounded by mosquitoes. *I want to marry you, Charlotte.*

"Luke. Luke?" Charlotte waited, and Luke realized he had missed everything she just said while he pictured the engagement ring he wanted to get her.

"Huh? Oh, sorry. What?"

"I said I'm not going back to St. Louis." Charlotte smiled.

Confusion settled on his face. "They didn't give you your job back? Are they crazy? Weren't you able to prove that it wasn't your fault?"

"I was, and they did. But I turned in my resignation." She paused. "And I sold my condo. I kept my Mazda, though – because I do love that car, even though it isn't the least bit practical for living out here in the sticks." Charlotte loved teasing him about being a hillbilly living in the boonies, even though she would never actually describe him that way in seriousness.

Luke tickled her ribs. "The sticks, eh? And just where do you plan on living now that you sold your condo?"

"I will definitely be living in the sticks." And with that admission, Luke couldn't say anything. Instead, kissed her again. This time, joyfully and exuberantly and full of the excitement he was practically jumping with.

"But what about your work? What will you do?" In her note, she had explained to him her need to use her abilities and her experience. He knew her well enough to know that hadn't changed with her short visit to her old life.

Charlotte was excited to explain. "Well, the church I went to in St. Louis was in the middle of a search for a new pastor. And they were using a pastoral search firm. I never knew that there was such a thing. For a large church, hiring a pastor is essentially like hiring a CEO. I called some people and got an interview with Ascension Ministry Staffing – one of the top pastoral search firms in the country. They want to keep me on retainer for interviews and screenings, based on my experience in the world of corporate recruiting. In fact, they already knew who I was, and my friend Joe gave me a glowing recommendation. It's perfect. They said I can live wherever and fly to wherever a candidate is located in order to interview them."

"That's amazing, Charlotte. I'm so happy for you! I'm so happy for us. You get to stay in Minden!" He picked her up and spun her around, soaking in the sound of her laughter.

EPILOGUE

Charlotte wrapped the long wool scarf around her neck. It was soft and warm and perfect for the chilly autumn evening waiting for her at the Harvest Festival. She grinned when Luke's truck ambled up the rutted drive. The same hunter green truck covered in mud had greeted her at the QuikStop on her first day in Minden. Seeing it meant seeing Luke, and that always gave her a fluttery thrill. Luke picked her up at the cottage and they drove into town. After he parked, Luke took her hand as they headed into the park located at the end of Main Street. They wandered through the stands, sipping on hot apple cider. Young children ate caramel apples with sticky fingers and faces.

Luke lifted her onto the trailer for the hayrack

ride, and she leaned against his strong frame in the corner of the ride. It felt natural to be there. In a way she hadn't felt when she'd returned to St. Louis, coming back to Minden had felt like coming home. She'd been back a few weeks and had never been happier. Her growing closeness with Luke was rivaled only by her growing relationship with Christ. And her new friends, Ruth, Chrissy, and Mandy had greeted her with open arms.

Charlotte and Luke chatted with Mark and shared a funnel cake for dinner as the sun dipped below the buildings of Main Street. Luke suggested they try the maze. Charlotte resisted, but agreed once he promised her that they wouldn't get lost. A few turns into the maze, Luke tugged on her hand and stopped her. Her brow furrowed, she looked back at him. The end of the maze was that way and they hadn't made a wrong turn yet. Luke took a deep breath and dropped to one knee. Looking up at her, he spoke in strong, confident tones. Charlotte's gasp was swallowed by the cool air and the shriek of children on the other side of the haybales lining the maze path.

"Charlotte Marie Walters. I love you more than I ever thought I would be able to love someone again. The weeks without you here were horrible. Knowing that you were somewhere, fighting a fight without me. I want to stand beside you and support you. And I want to come home to you every night." She warmed at the thought of sharing a home with Luke. Perfect, strong, stubborn Luke. "After Rachel died, I never thought I would find love again. I never imagined someone like you would invade this town, my life, and my heart the way you have. You're my miracle, sweetheart, and I love you beyond measure. Would you marry me?

Tears ran down her cheeks, leaving icy tracks as they cooled. "Lucas Brand, I never imagined I would find something more than a place to rest in Minden. And when I saw you ogle my car at the QuikStop, I thought you were some teenage kid." She sniffled and laughed at the memory. "I'm so glad I was wrong on both counts. I found God here. I found you and Miss Ruth. Most of all," she continued, "I found myself here. Oh Luke, I love you, too!" She softened her tone, serious now. "I'm so disappointed I never got to know Rachel, because her legacy has changed my life." Luke nodded, acknowledging his first wife and the love they had shared. Charlotte often thanked God for Rachel and for what she and Ruth had done for Luke. He wouldn't be the man she loved without them. When Charlotte continued, her smile grew. "You are home to me and so is Minden. Absolutely nothing would make me happier than being your wife." With a grin, Luke fit the ring on her finger and she pulled him up and into her arms. She tipped her head up to his and he kissed her deeply, tipping her back in a dramatic bend as joy overwhelmed them both.

Luke was the first to speak when they finally came up for air, both laughing. He wiggled his eyebrows at her and gave a crooked grin. "Now, how long of an engagement are we talking here, sweetheart?"

CHRISSY SMILED and handed Roy his apple cider. *Finally, a break in the action.* Bud and Janine's booth at the Harvest Festival had been busy since she set it up and started handing out the warm drinks. At lunch today, Todd admitted that Luke was proposing to Charlotte tonight. She caught Todd watching her from the apple bobbing station across the sidewalk. Pointing to the maze, he mouthed "It's happening." Luke and Charlotte had disappeared into the haybale maze a few minutes ago.

She gave a small smile. Charlotte and Luke

deserved every bit of happiness. It was a miracle they found each other. And the way God was working in Charlotte's life to use her unique talents in a new way? Amazing.

It had only been in the last year or two that Chrissy was on speaking terms with God anyway. She tried to remember what He had done since then. Her life was good. Her fake smiles had slowly become genuine, most of the time. So where was this discontent coming from? She glanced back at Todd, his mouth wide opening, demonstrating for a young boy the proper apple bobbing technique. She laughed when he gave a loud "Ahhhh" and shook his head side to side.

"You look like a labrador retriever!" she called with a giggle.

Todd flashed a smile at her, then made his way across the sidewalk.

"They say dogs are woman's best friend." He stuck his tongue out and panted, tipping his head as if asking to be petted.

"Pretty sure that's diamonds," she responded dryly, fighting back a laugh. He was her best friend, actually. Todd always made her laugh. He also happened to make her stomach do backflips, and, unfortunately, seemed completely content just being friends.

Todd shrugged. "Personally, I'd go for the dog."

Chrissy caught familiar movement out of the corner of her eye. Luke and Charlotte exited the maze, Charlotte tucked under Luke's arm and leaning into him. The joy evident on their faces and their close embrace made Charlotte twinge with envy. Todd got their attention and waved a hand. "Looks like congratulations are in order. Come on, let's go see them." Todd reached back and grabbed her hand, pulling her toward their friends.

Can Chrissy and Todd go from friends to more? Find out in Winter Wishes, Book 2 in the Main Street Minden Series.

UNTITLED

Note to Readers

To my readers - thank you for picking up (or down-loading!) this book and giving me a chance. I look forward to sharing the stories of many more characters with you - especially the ones in Minden.

As any author can tell you, reviews are incredibly important to our success as an author. Please take a minute to leave a review! Also, you can learn more about my upcoming projects at my website: www.taragraceericson.com. You can also get a free story by signing up for my newsletter. Follow me on Facebook or Instagram for chances to win advanced reader copies, see sneak peeks of upcoming books, and my book recommendations or random thoughts!

I have always devoured books as though they provide sustenance. The books I chose were not always edifying. As much as I love a good Amish or "Old West" romance novel filled with stories of love and faith and family; I became frustrated that so much of the Christian Romance genre was dominated with stories of another time period - as though it is impossible to live out your faith in the world of today, or find romance without going back in time. So I started writing my own. I hope you enjoyed it and that it was a worthwhile use of your time. I pray it encouraged you in your faith and your struggles.

ACKNOWLEDGMENTS

First and foremost, to my Savior, the Author of life - You are so, so good. The twists and turns of my life so far have led me closer to You and Your purpose. I never thought I'd be here, but You can do so much more than we ask or imagine.

Thank you to my friends and family, without whose support and encouragement, I would have given up a long time ago. Thanks especially to my trusted advanced readers, Gabbi, Charla, and Lynn - your feedback was invaluable in making this novel less terrible!

To Jessica, our new friendship is a wonderful blessing. Thank you for your constructive feedback and for going on this journey with me.

To Carla, I am so thankful for you! The hours we get to spend together are some of my favorites!

To my mother - the editor. I love our talks and how our relationship as evolved over the years. Your story inspires me every day and I strive to live up to your example as a wife, mother, and follower of Christ.

To all of my author friends - those in ACFW, 20Books, the Writing Gals and others, thank you for the knowledge you've shared so freely. I wouldn't be here without your support. Keep writing!

Lastly, to the baristas at my local Starbucks, who tolerated my presence for hours - and my insistence on a real mug - thank you for providing the caffeine and the background noise so critical to my creative process.

ABOUT THE AUTHOR

Tara Grace Ericson lives in Missouri with her husband and two sons. She studied engineering and worked as an engineer for many years before embracing her creative side to become a full-time author. Her first book, Falling on Main Street, was written mostly from airport waiting areas and bleak hotel rooms as she traveled in her position as a sales engineer.

She loves cooking, crocheting, and reading books by the dozen. Her writing partner is usually her black lab - Ruby - and a good cup of coffee or tea. Tara unashamedly watches Hallmark movies all winter long, even though they are predictable and cheesy. She loves a good "happily ever after" with an engaging love story. That's why Tara focuses on writing clean contemporary romance, with an emphasis on Christian faith and living. She wants to encourage her readers with stories of men and women who live out their faith in tough situations.

BOOKS BY TARA GRACE ERICSON

The Main Street Minden Series

Falling on Main Street

Winter Wishes

Spring Fever

Summer to Remember

Kissing in the Kitchen: A Main Street Minden Novella

The Bloom Sisters Series

Hoping for Hawthorne